"Can't we take Miss Anna flying, Daddy?"

Hoyt glanced in the rearview mirror to see Jess leaning forward, her face pleading. As he watched, his daughter's gaze shifted briefly from him to Anna. "Please?"

Anna's gaze fastened on to his for a second, then she turned to look back at Jess. "Are *you* asking me to go up in that plane, sweetie?" Hoyt held his breath as Jess hesitated.

"Yes."

It might have been the softest whisper Hoyt had ever heard, but it was definitely an answer. Jess was talking to Anna.

But the joyful relief that surged up in him was mixed with fear. Everything he'd prayed for hinged directly on what Anna did next.

He caught her green eyes with his and tried his best to communicate silently. *Please, Delaney. This matters. Please don't say no. Not now.*

He could tell Anna understood him. She instantly went about five shades paler, but she managed a choppy nod. "Well, fine, then. Since *you're* asking me, Jess."

Hoyt's heart swelled with gratitude—and guilt. "Are you sure?"

"No," she muttered, pushing open the truck door. "But I'm doing it anyway."

Laurel Blount lives on a small farm in Middle Georgia with her husband, David, their four children, a milk cow, dairy goats, assorted chickens, an enormous dog, three spoiled cats and one extremely bossy goose with boundary issues. She divides her time between farm chores, homeschooling and writing, and she's happiest with a cup of steaming tea at her elbow and a good book in her hand.

Books by Laurel Blount

Love Inspired

A Family for the Farmer
A Baby for the Minister
Hometown Hope

Hometown Hope

Laurel Blount

ISBN-13: 978-1-335-47930-3

Hometown Hope

This edition published by arrangement with Love Inspired Books.

www.Harlequin.com

Printed in U.S.A.

He healeth the broken in heart,
and bindeth up their wounds.
—*Psalms* 147:3

For the fabulous four: Rebecca, Jackson,
Joanna and Levi—with all my love.

Chapter One

Uh-oh.

Anna Delaney stopped doodling frowny faces and dollar signs in the margin of her notebook and tilted her head, listening. Sure enough, an all-too-familiar rustling was coming from her bookstore's storage room. Smothering a groan, Anna dropped her head down on the checkout counter with a thump.

The possum was back.

How was that even possible? Two weeks ago, when she'd finally caught the skinny-tailed varmint in a live trap baited with peanut butter, she'd driven him fifteen miles out into the country before setting him free. She hadn't seen him since, and she'd hoped he was the one problem related to this store that she'd actually managed to solve.

Apparently not. The animal must've liked living in Pine Valley, Georgia, a lot more than she did.

Anna heaved a sigh and started to get up. Then she pressed her lips together, sat back down and picked up her pen.

On second thought, that possum could stay right where he was.

She always kept that door locked, so there was no way he could sneak in here or into her loft apartment upstairs. Another early June thunderstorm was brewing, and if the stubborn animal wanted to spend his Friday night nice and dry amid boxes of paperbacks, Anna wasn't going to argue with him.

Pretty soon he wouldn't be her problem anymore. Today, after months of sleepless nights and unanswered prayers, Anna had finally come to terms with the inevitable. Pages, Pine Valley's one and only bookstore, was going out of business.

She still couldn't quite wrap her mind around how this had happened. Pneumonia had ended her father's long struggle with Alzheimer's only three months ago. Now this store—the retired principal's legacy to his beloved community—was fading away, too. And his only daughter, a woman with two completed university degrees and three-fourths of a PhD, hadn't been able to stop it.

It was downright depressing—not to mention humiliating. And to make matters worse, her hopes that her struggles were going unnoticed had been dashed this afternoon.

The minute Trisha Saunders had walked through the door, Anna had known something was up. Her former high school classmate owned Buds and Blooms, the flower shop next door, but she'd never bothered to visit Pages before.

Trisha had her five-year-old and several of his day care classmates in tow.

"Go find a book for Jimmy," she'd instructed her son.

"I've been so swamped at work I totally forgot to pick up a birthday present for him, and I don't have time to run to a toy store now. A book will have to do. The rest of you can help look, and then we'll go on to the party." The children had begun pulling books off the shelves, but when Anna had headed over to help, Trish had stopped her with one perfectly manicured hand. "Don't worry about them, Anna. They can find the book by themselves. I want to talk to you about something."

Then she'd tugged Anna aside and made an offer on the bookstore. Or more accurately, the building that housed it.

Trisha's tone had been almost as insulting as the amount she'd offered.

"You won't get a better deal," Trisha had said, casting an appraising look around as the children played a shrieking game of hide-and-seek among the shelves. "This space needs a lot of updating. I wouldn't touch it myself if our two buildings weren't attached. Besides, everybody knows you're holding on by your fingernails. Now that your dad's dead, why not just sell this store and move on with your life?"

Now that your dad's dead. The nonchalant way Trisha had tossed off that horrible phrase cracked across Anna's sore heart like a slap.

She doesn't know, Anna had reminded herself. Trisha's parents were still both living. She had no idea what it felt like to lose the only family you had in the whole world.

"Obviously running a business isn't your strong suit, Anna," Trisha had continued in a patronizing tone. "Isn't there something else you'd rather be doing? I mean, weren't you taking some high-level university classes or something before your dad got sick?"

"I was working toward a PhD in literature. Well, British literature, actually. I—"

"Whatever." Trisha had interrupted Anna's explanation with an impatient shrug. "Sell the store to me, and you can go back and finish that up. It's the perfect solution all the way around. So, how soon can you have all this junk cleared out?"

Anna had felt a flash of indignation. Books weren't junk. But she'd held her tongue. Based on her personal experience—and her sales figures—most people in Pine Valley agreed with Trisha. "I haven't the foggiest idea."

"Well, don't take too long. I need to get all this settled before my *other* new addition comes along." Trish had patted her round baby bump with a self-satisfied smile.

Remembering that little smirk, Anna scribbled so hard that the point of her pen tore through the notebook paper.

Back in high school Trisha had scraped by academically, spending her weekends partying while Anna had spent almost all her time with her nose stuck in some textbook. Now Trisha was balancing a booming business with a picture-perfect growing family. Meanwhile Anna "Brainy" Delaney, valedictorian and triumphant winner of the Hayes scholarship, was living alone above a bankrupt bookstore, sharing her peanut butter with a possum.

Life certainly hadn't turned out the way she'd expected.

A sudden clap of thunder boomed, causing the walls of the hundred-year-old building to shudder. Glancing up from her scribbles, Anna caught a quick glimpse of Pine Valley's town square through the wide store window before the downpour started. She sighed and set down her pen.

She'd better crank up the dehumidifiers. Damp seeped into the cracks of this old building, warping books and condensing on the inside of the windows.

So much for her idea of staying open late in the hopes of drumming up an extra sale or two. Nobody would be out in this weather. She might as well lock up, go upstairs and start researching all the logistics involved in closing a bookstore.

She sure hoped that would turn out to be easier than running one.

Anna flipped the sign in the door's window to Closed and twisted the grudging bolt into place. After flicking off the lights, she picked her way through the dim store, pausing at the checkout counter just long enough to snag an empty coffee mug and, after a second's guilty hesitation, her bookmarked novel.

She wouldn't read long, she promised herself. Just a few minutes.

A half hour, tops.

Blam! Blam-blam-blam!

Halfway up the steps to her apartment, Anna whirled around as another flash of lightning lit up the darkened store. A man stood at the door, his face pressed against the glass, pounding on it with one clenched fist.

Anna yelped, dropping both her coffee mug and her book. The lightning flickered again, and when she caught her second glimpse of the man, her fear morphed into annoyance.

Oh, for crying out loud.

That was Hoyt Bradley. Since the man had never voluntarily opened a book in his life, Anna had no idea what he was doing banging on the door of a bookstore in the middle of a storm, but he wasn't going to kill her.

Well, not unless he was planning to aggravate her to death.

Hoyt made an impatient what-are-you-waiting-for gesture through the glass, and Anna rolled her eyes. Then she stepped over her broken mug and stalked back down the steps toward the door.

Hoyt had always been as stubborn as a mule. She didn't know what he'd come for, but he wouldn't leave until he got it. She might as well deal with him now. Anna flipped the lights back on and slid the bolt free.

Hoyt lunged into the shop, rivers of rainwater sluicing off his broad used-to-be-a-football-star shoulders. "Is she here?"

"You could've given me a heart attack banging on the door like that! And watch what you're doing! You're flinging water all over my Jane Austens." Anna grabbed one sodden shirtsleeve and tried to tug Hoyt away from the classics she'd hopefully arranged in a display near the entryway.

It was like trying to move a boulder. Hoyt didn't budge. *"Is she here, Anna?"*

"Is who here? Hoyt, seriously, you're soaked through, and you're getting water *everywhere.* Do you even own an umbrella?"

Since he obviously wasn't going to move, she'd better scoot the cardboard display stand out of the puddle he was creating.

"Anna, *please.*" As she turned away, Hoyt reached out and caught her upper arms, his wet hands chilling her bare skin. Her pulse skittered out of rhythm as memories flooded her brain.

She'd sat knee to knee with Hoyt Bradley every afternoon for eight months during her junior year in high school. Every single time his leg had accidentally brushed hers, her pulse had done the same ridiculous thing.

She wasn't sixteen anymore. She should have outgrown this nonsense.

Apparently she hadn't.

She glared up at him, her cheeks stinging hot, poised to twist out of his grip and give him a generous piece of her mind. What she saw brought her up short.

Hoyt's handsome, square-jawed face was pale, and raw fear widened his hazel eyes. Right then all those silly oh-my-word-he-touched-me butterflies fluttering in Anna's stomach fell horribly still. Something was wrong.

Nothing scared Hoyt Bradley.

"Where's Jess?" Hoyt ground out the question, and Anna's eyes widened. He was looking for his five-year-old daughter.

"I—I don't know," Anna stammered. "I haven't seen her. I mean, I saw her for a little while this afternoon. She was with that group of kids Trisha was taking to Jimmy McAllister's party."

"When?"

"I…I don't remember, exactly."

"Think."

He was still holding her arms. She wished he wasn't, because it made thinking a whole lot harder. She swallowed and tried to focus.

"They came in a little after three, and they stayed

until almost four thirty." During which time they'd pretty much destroyed her children's area, while Trisha tried to convince Anna to accept one-third of her building's value. "What's going on?"

"Did you *see* Jess leave with Trisha?"

Anna did her best to remember. Finally she shook her head. "I assumed she did. But of course, she's so quiet—" She broke off, darting a quick look up into Hoyt's face.

Everybody in Pine Valley knew that little Jess Bradley hadn't spoken a single word since her mother's death almost three years ago. Everybody also knew it wasn't a topic you discussed with Hoyt.

"Anyway," Anna continued after an awkward second, "she must have gone with the rest of them because she's not here now. I've been all alone for the past couple of hours. Oh, no." The worried lines grooved into Hoyt's face suddenly made sense. "Is Jess *missing*?"

Missing. His Jess.

Fear slammed into Hoyt like a three-hundred-pound linebacker. *Let me find her, Lord,* he prayed silently. *And keep her safe until I do. Please.*

"All I know is I can't find her. I went to pick her up at the McAllisters', and she wasn't there. Trisha took Jess from day care with the rest of the kids, but she can't seem to remember where she lost track of her." He couldn't wrap his mind around that, but right now he had to stay focused on finding his little girl.

He'd deal with Trisha Saunders later.

"Oh, Hoyt." Anna's ice-green eyes warmed with sympathy, but the change didn't make him feel better. If Anna Delaney was feeling sorry for him, things were even worse than he thought. "You must be worried out of your mind."

Yeah. Pretty much. He ran one hand impatiently through his wet hair. "I thought she might be here with you. She likes this place." That was an understatement. Jess was crazy in love with this store. She tugged him in here every time they passed by, and she never wanted to leave.

That was why he'd been hoping…

"She's not here, Hoyt." Anna's forehead was creased with concern. "Do you think you should go talk to the sheriff?"

"I'm headed there next." He couldn't believe this had happened. If Marylee were still alive…

But she wasn't. The grief he'd lived with for three long years stabbed him like a broken rib. It did that sometimes. Mostly it was just a dull ache these days, but every now and then it flared back up and sucker punched him.

Especially when he felt like he was flunking single fatherhood big time.

Like now.

But he couldn't waste precious time feeling guilty. Not until he found Jess.

"I'll go talk to Sheriff Towers. If you see her—" He'd started to turn toward the door, but he froze, listening. His eyes locked with Anna's. "I thought you said you were alone."

"I am. That's nothing. Just a silly possum I can't keep out of my storage room."

"Maybe not." Hoyt shouldered past Anna and headed in the direction of the noise.

There was only one door at the back of the store. He

tried the knob, but it was locked. He shot a questioning look at Anna.

"I'll unlock it." Anna moved to the checkout area and started opening and shutting drawers, riffling through their contents with hurried fingers. "But I'm telling you, it's nothing but that stupid possum. I can't get rid of him."

Hoyt's fear, mixed with his newfound hope, made him vibrate with impatience. He needed to know right now if Jess was in that room. "Could you hurry this up, Anna?"

"Hang on a second. I know the key's here somewhere because I used it just a few hours ago. I moved some breakable items in there when the kids got wild playing hide-and-seek, and—oh!—" She stopped, her eyes wide. "I unlocked the door while they were here," she said slowly, "for just a few minutes."

That was all Hoyt needed to hear. He wasn't waiting for any key.

"Jess, baby, if you're in there, move to the back of the room. Okay?"

He reared back and kicked the door. The flimsy lock broke instantly, and the door flew so wide that it banged against the wall like a gunshot.

And there she was, his little girl, crouched on the floor. She blinked up at him like a startled baby owl.

Hoyt crossed the room in two strides and swept his daughter up into his arms. Pressing her against his chest, he closed his eyes, breathing in the familiar scent of her baby shampoo.

"Daddy's got you, honey. Are you all right?" Hoyt murmured the question raggedly against his daughter's wispy blond hair. She nodded against his chest, but

Hoyt pulled her gently away to check her over for himself. Her eyes, the blue of a robin's eggs, were wide, but she didn't seem to be hurt. He nestled her back against him, feeling her little fingers twining tightly into the fabric of his shirt.

Other than being a little spooked, Jess seemed all right.

Which meant everything else was all right.

Hoyt squeezed his eyes closed. *Thank You, God.*

As his heartbeat slowed back down into its regular gear, he opened his eyes. His gaze caught on the window across the room.

"Anna?"

"Hoyt, truly, I had no idea she was in there." Anna spoke from behind him, her voice shaking. He turned to look at her. She'd gone so pale that the half dozen freckles on her nose stood out like flecks of golden paint on a white wall. "She must have slipped in while I was talking to Trisha. I guess I was so distracted that I didn't notice her before I locked the door." Anna's worried gaze shifted to Jess. "Sweetie, I'm so, so sorry."

"Not your fault." Sure, he and Anna had been like oil and water ever since their big blowup back in high school, but Hoyt knew she'd never do anything like this on purpose. "This was nothing but a crazy accident." One that had almost given him a heart attack, but now that Jess was safely back in his arms, he was feeling a lot more forgiving. Hoyt drew in a deep breath and shifted Jess's weight on his arm. Might as well get this next part over with. "Speaking of crazy accidents, was that window over there already broken?"

"What? Yes. Three of the panes have been cracked forever, but—" Anna broke off and bit her lip as she studied her window. “Oh.” The damaged glass had fallen completely out of the frame and splintered on the floor, leaving gaping spaces behind. “Well, no. Not like that.”

That was what he’d been afraid of. “When I kicked the door in, the impact must have jarred the cracked panes loose.” He’d broken the door, too, but he didn’t feel as bad about that. It was a cheap hollow core not original to the building. He could get dozens of those down at the building supply store.

That window was a different story. Hoyt’s contractor brain kicked in. The watery-looking glass in the intact panes meant he was looking at an antique fixture. Not a standard size, either. It was going to be ridiculously expensive to repair, if he could even get glass to match, which was doubtful. The whole window would probably have to be replaced.

As he silently summed up the damages, gusts of wind blew in through the empty holes, bringing heavy splats of rain with them.

“Excuse me.” Anna made a worried noise as she brushed past him. She grabbed the flaps of a rain-spattered cardboard box and began tugging it away from the window.

“I’ll do that.” He reluctantly set Jess on her feet. “Stay put for a minute, pumpkin, okay?” He waited until she nodded and then made short work of moving boxes out of the danger zone while Anna hovered on the sidelines.

“Thanks,” she murmured. Opening one of the dampest boxes, she checked the contents. She made unhappy clucking sounds as she unpacked the books. She gave each one a quick once-over before stacking them on a nearby table.

Hoyt watched the process with a sense of confusion. There was at least six or seven hundred dollars' worth of structural damage in this room, but Anna was worrying over a box of wet books?

He'd never understand this woman.

Anna made it to the bottom of the box and sighed. "Most of these are okay. I might have to discount a couple for water spotting, but other than that, I don't think you did any real damage."

Hoyt waited, eyebrows lifted.

Nothing.

"Except for your busted window and door," he finally pointed out.

"Oh, right." Anna considered the broken glass. "There is that. Not that it really matters now," she muttered under her breath.

What did she mean by that? No telling. Hoyt shook his head.

Nope, he'd never understand Anna Delaney. Not in a million years.

He grabbed a broom leaning against the wall. "Hand me that dustpan there. I can't do much tonight because I need to get Jess on home to bed, but I can at least get this mess cleaned up a little."

"I can manage," Anna protested. He ignored her.

He swept up the broken glass and dumped it in the trash. Then he snagged some rags off a pile of cleaning products and wadded them into the empty panes. He was able to shut out the worst of the blowing rain, but just to be on the safe side, he shifted three more boxes of Anna's precious books farther from the window.

Mainly because he figured that if he didn't, Anna would do it the minute he left.

Then he picked Jess up and settled her back against his chest. "That's the best I can do for now. I'll be by first thing in the morning to take some measurements so I can get the materials I'll need for the repair."

"You're fixing it?" Anna looked so jittery at the idea that it was almost funny.

Almost.

"I'm a building contractor, Anna. Fixing things is what I do." That doubtful expression she was wearing was a little insulting. "Is that a problem? Because I can get somebody else to handle the repair, but I can't promise you when it'll happen. Summer's a busy season, and every man worth his salt is up to his elbows in work right now. But if you'd rather have somebody else fix this—"

"No! *You* fix Miss Anna's bookstore, Daddy. I don't want Miss Trisha to make this place go away."

A man's life could change on a dime. Hoyt had lived long enough and hard enough to know that firsthand. And when it did, for a second or two, time just sort of…stopped.

As he looked down at Jess, Hoyt could hear the ticking of the old clock on the wall of the bookstore and the flapping of the flimsy awnings Principal Delaney had paid some jackleg out-of-town guy to install on the front of the building. But as far as Hoyt was concerned, the whole world had narrowed down to a tiny girl in a pink T-shirt.

After three long years of silence, Jess had finally spoken.

Dr. Mills had assured him this would happen one

day, but he'd almost stopped hoping for it. Even the therapist had started to worry. He'd seen it in her eyes the last time he'd taken Jess to Atlanta for an appointment. Both of them knew the statistics for selective mutism, and they knew Jess's silence had dragged on way too long.

Act normal when it happens. The counselor's optimistic instructions replayed themselves in his head. *It's a delicate moment. Don't make a big deal out of it.*

Yeah, right. Turned out that was a lot easier to talk about than it was to do. He'd never been much of a crier, but right now his eyes were stinging like he'd been chopping onions.

"Wh—" His own voice came out so rusty that he had to clear his throat and try again. "What did you say, sweetheart?"

Jess put her small hands on each of his cheeks, tilting his head down until their foreheads bumped together. She looked deeply into his eyes. "Fix Miss Anna's bookstore, Daddy. Pretty please promise?"

Pretty please promise. His gut twisted as he remembered the last time he'd heard that cutesy phrase. The memory was sharp. He could almost smell that weird hospital odor again and see a smaller Jess's tear-streaked face.

The moment wasn't something he was likely to forget. It was the last time he'd heard his daughter speak… when she'd asked him to keep the promise he never should have made in the first place.

Mommy will get better, honey. I promise.

He shook off the memory. This time was different. This time Jess was asking for something he *could* do.

"Sure thing, baby. Daddy'll fix everything, don't you worry. This bookstore's not going anywhere. I promise."

Anna cleared her throat, but Hoyt jerked his head sharply and cut her a pleading look.

Not now.

Anna must've read his face correctly. She bit her lip. "We should talk, Hoyt." Her voice was carefully calm, but her expression wasn't.

"We will. I have to get Jess home now, but I'll come back tomorrow. We can talk everything over then." He didn't wait for her to respond.

He had no idea why Principal Delaney's run-down old bookstore had been the key to unlock Jess's speech when nothing else had worked, but he wouldn't waste time wondering about it. The game he'd been losing had finally changed, and Hoyt had possession of the ball for the first time in three years.

Tomorrow he'd find out exactly what that funny expression on Anna's face meant, and he'd work his way around whatever problem was standing between him and the end zone.

Whatever it was, he already knew it didn't stand a chance.

Chapter Two

At six thirty the next morning, Anna set her devotional book down on the counter and refilled her coffee mug. She was going to need all the caffeine she could get today.

She hadn't slept well. Yesterday's events had played on an endless loop in her mind. Trisha's mean-spirited offer on the building, followed by Hoyt's frantic visit and the horrifying discovery that Anna had locked an emotionally traumatized five-year-old in her storage room.

Then the astonishment of Jess speaking. That was the memory that got to her most of all. The incredulous joy on Hoyt's face… She still got choked up, thinking about it.

The Bradley family had been through a lot. The whole of Pine Valley had sympathized with Hoyt in his grief and worried over Jess's long silence.

Especially Anna's father. He'd written Jess and Hoyt's names on the very top of the prayer list he'd kept tucked in his Bible. Her father loved everybody in his small town, but Jess Bradley held an extra special place in his heart. He'd always considered the little girl's love of books one of his biggest successes as an educator.

Before his memory had completely failed him, her father had told her proudly about how Hoyt's wife had brought Jess in for story times and other special bookstore events.

"Neither I nor his teachers could ever get Hoyt interested in literature, but we did manage to reach Marylee Sherman. She was an avid reader, and she was doing her best to make sure that baby of theirs loved books, too. It's a shame how things work out sometimes. It truly is."

Her father would have been so pleased to see how Marylee's efforts continued to pay off. Jess's passion for books had grown until it rivaled Anna's own. Come to think of it, because of Jess, Anna had sold more books to Hoyt Bradley over the past couple of years than to anybody else in Pine Valley.

Her father would've chuckled over that.

Anna might have appreciated the irony a lot more herself if it hadn't meant seeing Hoyt on a regular basis. Even after all these years, Hoyt Bradley made her feel… uncomfortable.

She hadn't always felt that way. Once upon a time she'd actually *tried* to run into Hoyt, hanging around hallways where she knew he had classes, making long detours by the athletes' boisterous lunch table, hoping he'd look up and say hi.

That was the sort of thing that happened when you were shy and socially invisible, and your beloved English teacher asked you to tutor the local football star. Anna's job had been to keep Hoyt eligible to play, but she hadn't stopped there. She'd boosted Hoyt's GPA enough that he'd qualified for a college football scholarship.

Then copies of senior exams had been discovered in the gym locker room, and all eyes had turned on Anna. After all, people had said, as the principal's daughter, she had access to the school after hours, and Hoyt was…well, *Hoyt Bradley.* Any girl, especially a nerdy bookworm like Anna, would be willing to do whatever a guy like that asked her to do.

It all made perfect sense.

It just wasn't true.

Anna had no idea how Hoyt had managed to get those test keys, but whatever he'd done, he'd done without her help. To be fair he'd tried to make that clear. He'd told everyone that Anna had nothing to do with the theft. But since he'd stopped short of making a public confession of his own guilt, most people had simply assumed he was covering for her.

There was some irony for you. Hoyt was the actual guilty party, but in the end, he'd come off looking like some chivalrous hero, while she looked like…well…

A lovestruck dork.

Which, if she were brutally honest with herself, was uncomfortably close to the truth.

A rapping on the door startled her out of her thoughts. She glanced up to see Hoyt peering at her from the sidewalk.

Anna shot an alarmed look at the antique clock on the wall. She'd known she'd have to deal with Hoyt at some point today, but what was he doing here at this hour? It wasn't even 7:00 a.m. On a *Saturday.* And she was wearing her rattiest yoga pants and an oversize green T-shirt with I'd Rather Be Reading scrawled across the front in glittery pink script.

Plus, she had the kind of curly hair that had to be beaten into submission every morning, and she hadn't even made her first attempt yet. She probably looked like some cartoon character who'd just been struck by lightning. Still, considering she'd locked the man's daughter in her storage room yesterday, she couldn't exactly shoo him away.

Besides, she'd been the accidental witness to an incredibly emotional moment last night. When Hoyt had heard his daughter's voice for the first time in way too long, she'd seen the man's heart hanging out. He was probably feeling vulnerable himself today, facing her after a moment like that.

Anna set down her mug, took a deep, calming breath and headed in his direction. She unlocked the door and opened her mouth to say something friendly and reassuring.

She didn't get the chance.

"You trying out a new look, Delaney?" Hoyt gave her a quick once-over and grinned. "I like it. You should wear your hair like that all the time."

As he shouldered past her into the store, Anna could feel her cheeks heating up. As usual, Hoyt Bradley was poking fun at her.

This man wasn't vulnerable. He was impossible.

"My Saturday hours are posted right there on the window. I don't open until ten today. I'm aware that reading goes against the whole caveman thing you've got going on, but you really should give it a try sometime."

He raised an eyebrow at her tone and then shrugged.

"Sorry about that." He didn't sound particularly sorry, but then Hoyt never did. "Some of us cavemen have to get to work early."

He did look ready for work. He was wearing a rust-colored shirt paired with khaki work pants and boots. An embroidered sign on his shirt pocket read Bradley Builders in black script. His dark hair was damp from a shower, and he smelled like some kind of foresty aftershave.

He made her feel like a slacker.

Whistling cheerfully, he paused to pour himself a mug of coffee from the machine behind the counter. "If you want that window and door fixed anytime soon, I need to take some measurements before I hit the building supply store this morning." He vanished into the storeroom, filched coffee in hand.

The instant he was out of sight, Anna went straight for the heavy-duty rubber bands she kept in a drawer at the checkout counter and attempted some emergency hair management.

Hoyt Bradley hadn't changed a bit since high school. She could almost feel her blood pressure going up.

She'd barely finished corralling her uncooperative hair into a messy ponytail when Hoyt reemerged from the storeroom. He retracted the tape measure in his hand and stuffed a torn scrap of paper in the breast pocket of his shirt. "I'm done. I can get the door fixed today, but I'm going to have to special-order the window, and that'll take a while. I'll board up the gap for you when I swing back by."

More Hoyt was the last thing she needed. "Don't worry about it. I can rig up something to keep the rain out."

"Rain's not all you want to keep out. You don't want somebody breaking in."

"In Pine Valley? I doubt that'll be a problem. Besides, there's nothing in here to steal except books."

Hoyt paused. For the first time since she'd opened the door, he looked serious. "About that. How bad is it?"

Something about his tone put Anna on alert. "How bad is what?"

"Are you carrying a lot of debt or is it just a cash flow problem?" Confused, she frowned at him, and he made an impatient noise. "The *bookstore*, Anna. How deep in the hole are you?"

Typical Hoyt, standing there, asking nosy questions as if he had every right to know. Well, she wasn't sharing. For one thing, her finances were none of his business.

And for another thing, she'd already been embarrassed enough for one morning, thank you very much.

"That's a bit personal, don't you think?"

Hoyt sighed and looked at his watch. "I think you never could give a guy a straight answer. I don't have time to get into all this right now anyway. I've got a job site to get to. We'll have to hash it out later. How about after work? That good for you? You could come over to my house for supper."

The man was unbelievable. "I don't think so."

"Why not? I'm serious, Anna. Me and you need to talk. You don't have anything more exciting lined up for tonight. Do you?"

It was something about the offhand way he tacked on the question and the humorous twinkle in his eye as he asked it. Like he already knew she'd be sitting at home alone on a Saturday night reading a book, just like always.

That happened to be true. But the fact that Hoyt Bradley knew it irritated her, and the words came out before she could stop herself.

"It's *you and I*."

"What?"

"*You and I* need to talk. Not *me and you*. I must have told you that at least a million times back in high school."

Hoyt stared for a second. Then he laughed and shook his head. "Still dishing out the Annatude. I guess some things never change."

Annatude. She'd forgotten about the word he'd made up back in high school. It had been their little inside joke, and she'd actually thought it was cute. For a while.

Until she'd realized that the joke was on her.

She lifted her chin. "Your grammar certainly hasn't changed."

Hoyt glanced at his watch and made an impatient noise. "Look, I really don't have time for all this right now, Anna, so let's cut to the chase. I know you don't like me much, okay? I get that, but this isn't about me. This is about Jess."

He was right. She didn't like him much. She also didn't like being steamrolled, so she'd been prepared to dig in her heels and stand her ground.

Right up until that last sentence.

She hesitated, torn between her irritation with Hoyt and her concern for his daughter. The concern won out. "What about Jess?"

"We'll talk about it tonight over supper." The corner of Hoyt's mouth twitched. "Me and you. Say, around six thirty? Don't expect a lot of bells and whistles, though. I'm not much of a cook, but I'll come up with something. You could bring some dessert if you want. You used to make a pretty stellar brownie if I remember right."

That was the wrong memory for him to bring up. Remembering the long afternoons she'd spent baking those sad little I-have-a-crush-on-you brownies still made her cringe.

That clinched it. No way was she was going to Hoyt Bradley's house for dinner. She opened her mouth to tell him so.

He must have read her expression, because he spoke before she could. "Anna, Jess is all I have. She finally talked last night after all these years, and I want—" His voice roughened, and he waited a second before continuing. "I'm going to do everything I can to make sure she keeps on talking. I know this isn't your problem, and I'm really sorry to bug you. But somehow you and this store of yours have gotten tangled up in my situation, so I'd appreciate it a lot if you'd take the time to talk with me about it. At my house. Tonight."

Jess is all I have. Anna chewed on her lower lip. She knew what it was like to have only one person in the whole world left to love. She also knew how it felt when that person slipped away from you into a place you couldn't access, no matter how desperately you wanted to.

She was going to kick herself for this later, but—

"Okay."

"Please, Anna, I—" Hoyt stopped short. For once in her life, she'd thrown him off-balance. *"Okay?"*

"Yes. I'll come."

Hoyt blinked a couple of times. "I really appreciate that. I guess I'll see you tonight."

"Right." They considered each other for an awkward second or two, and then Hoyt nodded and headed out of the store toward his truck.

Anna relocked the door behind him, her heart skipping nervously. Glancing up, she caught Hoyt studying her from the cab of the truck.

Their eyes connected, and she realized something. For probably the first and only time in their lives, she and Hoyt Bradley were thinking the exact same thing.

What on earth did I just get myself into?

Hoyt Bradley didn't spook easy, and he had his dad to thank for that. When you grew up in a house with a mean drunk, you learned early to cope with stuff that made most people turn tail and run.

So it made no sense for his palms to be sweaty when he reached for the doorknob at six thirty. On the dot.

Trust Anna Delaney to be right on time.

She was waiting in the shade of his deep front porch. Maybe she was trying to make up for that crazy outfit she'd been wearing earlier because now she looked like she was headed to a job interview at a funeral home. She had on a pink blouse buttoned up to the neck and gray slacks with a knife-blade crease down each leg. Somehow she'd even wrangled her unruly mop of hair into a prissy bun.

That must have taken some doing. And as far as Hoyt was concerned, it had been a big waste of time. He'd meant what he told her back in the bookstore. Her hair looked better the other way.

Still. Hoyt glanced down at his own rumpled blue

cotton shirt and jeans. All things considered, he probably could have stood a little sprucing up himself. She poked a foil-covered dish in his direction. "I brought dessert."

She'd taken his suggestion. Maybe this was going to be easier than he'd thought. "I hope it's those caramel brownies you used to make." She'd once bribed him to read an entire act of *Julius Caesar* by allowing him one bite per page.

"Sorry. Banana pudding."

He'd never much cared for bananas, and from that sharp twinkle in Anna's eye, she remembered. So much for easy. "Come on in."

She edged past him into his living room and threw a startled glance upward.

"Oh, *wow*." For a second or two she seemed to have forgotten he was standing there, which made the raw admiration in her voice mean even more. "This is incredible. I've never seen anything like it. Well, not in somebody's home, anyway. I feel like I just walked into a cathedral."

He'd designed the front room of his home with a vaulted ceiling that soared into a high point. Large triangular windows brought in the blue sky and tops of the old pecan trees in his yard. The back wall of the room was mostly glass, too, showcasing the sparkling pond he'd dug out in the back field.

He always enjoyed seeing people react to it, but nobody had ever commented that it looked like a church before now.

Strange, since he'd actually patterned this space after a sanctuary he'd helped build down in Savannah several years ago. He'd liked the way that building had brought in the outdoors, spotlighting God's creation rather than focusing on man-made curlicues. He thought he'd done a pretty fair job of copying that here.

Weird that Anna Delaney of all people would be the one who picked up on that.

"Thanks," he said simply.

Anna flushed and nodded awkwardly. She reached up a hand to tuck a straying lock of hair back into place. It flopped right back down as soon as she quit fussing with it.

Hoyt tried not to grin. For such an uptight girl, Anna sure had some wild hair. It was a glossy brown, and when she wore it down, it fell in loose spirals past her shoulders. She'd been fighting with it—and losing—as long as he'd known her.

"Where's Jess?" Anna dug in the bag she had looped over one elbow and produced a storybook. "I brought her something."

"She's not here." The immediate alarm in Anna's expression might have been funny if there hadn't been so much at stake. "We need to talk about some stuff she doesn't need to overhear, so I asked Bailey Quinn to take her out to Tino's for a pizza." Anna still looked uneasy, so he added, "That's okay, isn't it?"

She hesitated but then set her bag down on the table by the door and nodded. "I guess so." She tilted her head and sniffed. "Hoyt? Is something burning?"

He made it to the kitchen about the time the smoke alarm started going off. He opened the oven and drew out four charred lumps of garlic bread. Even by his low standards, they weren't salvageable.

Not a good start.

"If that's our dinner maybe we should skip right to dessert."

Anna had followed him and was leaning against the doorframe. Bombing the bread had served one purpose at least. She didn't look suspicious anymore. She looked amused.

"Nah, the lasagna's okay." Mainly because it had started out in the supermarket's frozen foods section. "I was trying to hurry this bread along. Me and the broil setting on this oven have a love-hate thing going on. I like it because it cooks stuff fast, but if you forget about it—" he gestured to the smoking lumps "—charcoal." The smoke alarm was still shrilling. "Could you hand me that broom?"

Anna picked it up. Instead of passing it to him, she upended it and poked the button on the ceiling alarm. The shrieking stopped.

When she saw him looking at her, she shrugged. "I went through a stir-fry period right after my dad died. I think I learned more about the smoke alarm in our old kitchen than I did about Chinese cooking."

That reminded him. Avoiding her eyes, Hoyt grabbed another pot holder and picked up the hot tinfoil pan of lasagna. "I'm sorry I missed Principal Delaney's funeral. I don't know how it slipped by me. I was planning to go, but then I never saw the announcement about it."

"There wasn't one."

"You should have announced it. I imagine pretty much everybody in town would have been there. Your dad was principal at the high school forever."

"No. I meant there wasn't a funeral."

Hoyt set the steaming pan down on the table and turned to look at her. "What?"

"I mean no public one." Anna avoided his gaze. "I just had a private memorial service. Only the minister and I were there."

"Why?"

"Well, Dad was sick for years and toward the end he didn't even recognize people. He was...disconnected. Nobody would've come." She glanced up at him and frowned. "What? Why are you looking at me like that?"

Hoyt realized he was staring at her with his mouth open. "Are you crazy? *Everybody* would have come. This whole town loved your dad."

She looked at him skeptically. "Then why didn't people visit him after he got sick? I mean, a few people did at first but then..." A spasm of pain crossed her face. "He didn't always know who people were, but he liked having visitors."

Regret settled on Hoyt's chest like a rock. That hurt in her eyes hit really close to home. "I wondered the same thing when Marylee got sick. People I expected to come by the hospital...didn't. Jacob Stone said it didn't mean they didn't care. He said that people have a hard time seeing somebody they love suffering."

She nodded. "He said the same thing to me." From the look on her face, she hadn't found it much more comforting than he had.

"I should have come by to see him. I'm sorry I didn't. Your dad was always good to me. Even after what happened senior year—"

"You know what? Let's not get into all that." Anna cut him off. "I'm here because you wanted to talk to me about Jess."

All right. If Anna wanted to leave the past in the past,

that was fine by him. “Okay. How about I say grace, and we’ll talk while we eat?”

They settled at the two places he’d set, and Hoyt reached across the table and took her hands in his.

He always held Jess’s hands when he said the blessing. He hadn’t thought about how inappropriate that might be from Anna’s point of view until he felt her jump. She didn’t pull away, though. Hoyt said possibly the shortest grace in the history of table blessing and released her.

She immediately put both hands in her lap. Okay, point taken. No more touching. In fact, from the look on her face, he’d better skip the small talk and get straight to the point of this visit before she ran right out the door.

He pried up a cheesy square of lasagna, set it on her plate and nudged the salad bowl in her direction. Showtime. “You know about Jess, right? How she stopped talking after her mother died?”

“Pine Valley’s a small town.” Anna frowned as she focused on transferring lettuce from the big bowl to the one by her plate. She didn’t lose a single leaf. “So, yes. I’d heard about that, and of course when she came into the store, I noticed she never said anything. Until last night.” Anna picked up her glass of sweet tea and looked at him over the rim. “Was that really the first time she’d—”

“It was.” Hoyt couldn’t help smiling at the memory.

“So is she still talking and everything?”

“To me, yeah. Just a little bit at first, but more and more. Only me, though. Not anybody else so far.” Hoyt tried using the salad tongs and ended up dumping about half the lettuce on the table. How did Anna manage these things? “But talking at all is a big step forward, according to her doctor. Today she asked me for some syrup for her pancakes. That probably happens every day in other people's houses, but it felt like Christmas morning over here, you know?"

Anna's expression softened. "I can imagine. I'm so glad she's all right, Hoyt. I felt awful about locking her in. I still can't believe I did that."

"Trust me. If there was ever a time when God took somebody's goof-up and turned it into gold, this was it. I called her therapist after I left the bookstore last night and told her about the whole thing. Dr. Mills thinks that maybe it was the trauma of being locked in combined with the relief of me coming to find her that finally encouraged her to talk. So since your mistake might turn out to be an answer to some pretty desperate prayers, I don't think I'd waste much time feeling bad about it, if I were you."

Anna studied him, a forkful of lasagna halfway to her lips, her expression unreadable. "I'm so glad," she repeated finally.

He probably wasn't going to get a better opening than that, so he'd better get this moving along. "Me, too. I just hope it lasts."

"What do you mean?"

He hated to say this out loud. He didn't even like thinking it. "Dr. Mills says that usually once kids like Jess—kids with selective mutism, the docs call them—start speaking, that's it. They keep on talking. But Jess's case has never been typical." As he repeated the therapist's words, he felt that familiar lump forming in his stomach. "So Dr. Mills can't say for sure what's going to happen. But the longer we keep her talking and the more people she starts to talk to, the more likely it is that this will be permanent." Hoyt paused, fumbling for the best way to say what he needed to say next.

He should've known he wouldn't have to spell things out for Anna Delaney.

"I'm assuming I'm here because there's some way you think I can help." Anna set down her fork and looked him in the eye. "You didn't have to go to all this trouble. I'll help Jess in any way I possibly can." Just as Hoyt relaxed with relief, Anna went on. "I just hope this doesn't have anything to do with my plans to close the bookstore."

His heart sank. "As a matter of fact, it does. Jess talked because of your dad's store, Anna. The therapist thinks it's all wrapped up with Marylee taking her there so much when she was little."

"But Jess was so young when Marylee died, Hoyt. How could she even remember that?"

"I asked the same thing, but the therapist said that on some level, she can. Dr. Mills said this goes down deep for Jess. That's why it's been such a challenge. But Jess is finally talking again, and that's all tied up with your store. If Pages closes right now, especially after I promised her it wouldn't, it could throw everything sideways."

Anna looked unhappy, but she shook her head. "I'm really sorry, Hoyt, but there's nothing I can do. Trust me, I've already tried everything to keep the store going. A blue-collar town like Pine Valley just isn't capable of supporting an independent bookstore."

"Your father seemed to do all right."

Anna's eyes flashed. He must have touched a nerve there. "My father devoted most of a good retirement pension and all his savings to keeping Pages afloat.

What assets he left had to be sold off to pay his medical bills. There's no money to subsidize the bookstore now."

"Look, I get it. When I inherited Bradley Builders from my own dad, it was circling the drain. But I built it back up, and it more than pays its way now." He leaned forward, holding her eyes with his own, willing her to believe him. "Maybe I could help you do the same thing with your place."

"You run a construction business, though. It's totally different, don't you think?"

Now it was Hoyt's turn to feel irritated. "I think business is business, Anna."

She studied him, her dark brows pulled together thoughtfully. "Where did you learn what to do to save your father's company? You never took any business classes back in high school. Did you go to night classes over at Fairmont Technical?"

Hoyt could see where this was going…the same direction things always went with Anna Delaney. Schooling. Books. Classrooms. Those were the only things she'd ever put much stock in.

"I learned on the job, by making mistakes and then having to figure out how to fix them." He could see her drawing back. His desperation made him reckless, and he pushed harder. "It's the best way to learn anything, if you ask me. Way better than reading some book."

He regretted the words the instant they were out of his mouth. You never insulted books in front of a Delaney. Anna's frown darkened, and he hurried on. "Look, things may not even be that bad. I talked to Trisha, and from what she said, your main issue seems to be that you've got no reach. You're basically selling to the same few people over and over again. You need to work on reconnecting with your customer base."

"You talked to Trisha Saunders about me?"

From the tone in Anna's voice, he was guessing he'd made another wrong step somewhere. This conversation was like walking through a minefield blindfolded. "Well, yeah. She owns the business right next door, so I knew she'd have a handle on how well the location works for foot traffic. And last night Jess said something about Trish wanting to close the bookstore. So, sure. I went and talked to her to get a feel for why you're having problems."

"I see." Anna set down her fork with a clink. She took her paper napkin out of her lap and refolded it beside her plate. "And did *Trish* offer you some valuable critiques about my business practices?"

Mainly what Trisha had offered were more of those flirty smiles she'd been aiming in his direction since Marylee died and a few snarky digs about the run-down condition of Anna's building. Hoyt had pieced together the rest of it on his own.

Probably not the best idea to go into any of that with Anna right now.

"My point is there's plenty you can do to bring in some more business, even without a lot of money to invest. Maybe you'll have to get a little more creative, but if you do some cross-promotions with other local business owners—"

Anna shook her head. "Look, Hoyt, I appreciate the offer, and I understand that you want to do whatever it takes to keep Jess talking. I do. But making the decision to close my father's bookstore wasn't something I did lightly. There's nothing that can be done at this point."

His frustration level bobbed upward. She wasn't listening to him, and he thought he knew why. "Nothing that *can* be done? Or nothing *I* can do?"

Anna sighed. "It's the same thing, Hoyt. Although, believe me, I do appreciate the fact that you, of all people, are trying to save a bookstore."

You. Of all people.

Something about that wry remark hit him a little too hard, and before he thought better of it, he hit back.

"Maybe I'm not much on books, Anna, but I'm turning down construction jobs right now. Trish Saunders didn't go to college, either, but that flower shop she started on a shoestring seems to be doing all right, too. Believe it or not, out here in the real world people learn some pretty useful things outside of a classroom. If you'd ever pulled your nose out of a book long enough, you might have figured that out already."

Anna's cheeks had turned fire-engine red. She stood. "I think we're done here."

Reading faces was another survival skill Hoyt had learned from dealing with his dad, so he knew there wasn't much point in trying to smooth things over. But he was desperate, so he took a shot anyway, as she turned and headed for the door.

"Anna, I'm sorry. Please wait."

For a second she hesitated, just long enough to get his hopes up. But then she squared her shoulders and went out the door.

Later, after putting Jess to bed, Hoyt sat on his back deck, listening to the chirring of the frogs down by the pond. He'd had more than his share of sleepless nights during the last few years, and he could tell he was gearing up for another one.

After all his careful planning, he'd blown things with Anna because he hadn't been able to keep a lid on his temper.

Delaney hadn't meant anything by that little jab. She'd just been cracking wise with him, the way they always did. It wasn't her fault she'd hit him on a sore spot. He shouldn't have overreacted.

His restless mind dredged up an uncomfortable memory. One afternoon in the heat of a pickup basketball game, a classmate had elbowed him in the ribs. Nothing new about that, but this time the blow just happened to land right where his father had slammed him the night before, when Hoyt had wedged himself in front of his cowering mother. Agony had exploded, and without even thinking about it, Hoyt had rammed the backside of his forearm into the other player's nose.

It had been nothing but a reflex on Hoyt's part, but the guy's nose bled all over the gym floor just the same as if Hoyt had set out to break it.

The incident had taught him a lesson. You couldn't allow your pain to splash over onto other people. It wasn't right.

He should have let Anna's little dig pass.

His cell phone buzzed, vibrating itself across the wooden table beside his rocking chair. He snatched it up and read the name on the screen. *Dr. Amanda Mills.* It was the call he'd been waiting for.

"Dr. Mills, thanks for getting back to me. I'm really sorry to bug you. I know you're busy taking care of your mom. How's she doing?"

"The doctors are still running tests. We don't know

much yet, except that she's had a massive stroke. And you can call me about Jess anytime, Hoyt. You know that." He did. The gray-haired pediatric therapist had been an answer to prayer.

He didn't want to waste her time, so he jumped right to the purpose of his call. "Jess is still talking only to me." He'd quizzed Bailey when she and Jess had returned from their pizza date, but no dice. According to Bailey, Jess had seemed content, and she'd eaten her weight in pizza, but she hadn't said a word. "What do you think that means?"

"Maybe nothing. Jess has always been on her own timetable. Most children with selective mutism start talking again in a matter of months, but Jess held out on us for years. This may run the same way. When she's good and ready, she'll talk to somebody else, and her social interactions will expand from there."

"Or?"

Dr. Mills sighed. "Or only talking to you could be her new normal. That's unlikely, but like I said, Jess is an unusual case."

Hoyt braced himself. "Any possibility she'll go back to not talking at all?"

"Hoyt—"

"Bottom line, Doc."

Dr. Mills hesitated for a second, but she'd always been honest with him. "Yes. There's always a possibility—a *small* possibility—of regression in cases like this."

"And if something happened that reminded her of how she felt back when her mom died, then that could up the chances of her going radio silent again? Couldn't it?"

Another heavy sigh. "Hoyt, I realize I've told you

this before, but please try to hear me this time. Jess's problems are *not your fault.*"

Yeah, right. "I broke a promise to her, and she stopped talking."

"It was a promise you couldn't possibly keep, involving a situation you couldn't control. You've said yourself nobody knew how serious your wife's illness was at first. Of course you promised Jess she'd get better. Any father would have promised a worried two-year-old the same thing. Stop being so hard on yourself."

Easier said than done. "Thanks, Dr. Mills. I appreciate your time."

"You're always welcome. For now, just keep doing what you've been doing, and we'll see what happens. I'm working Jess into my schedule the minute I get back home to Georgia. I'm confident we'll see even more amazing progress by that point."

"Me, too." Hoyt wasn't blowing smoke. He *was* confident.

He was going to do whatever it took to make sure Jess kept talking. First off, he needed to figure out how to get back on Anna's good side because he needed her on Jess's team. He'd probably better make a fresh pot of coffee and get started on that.

After tonight, winning Anna over wasn't going to be easy.

Chapter Three

Two days later Anna massaged her temples while the voice on the other end of the phone told her that her newest plan wasn't going to work any better than the old ones. "Are you *sure* there's no way for me to reapply for the grant I had before?" She listened as the university financial aid officer explained again that because she only lacked a year to finish her PhD, she was ineligible for the grant.

She'd heard him the first time, but she'd been hoping there might be some sort of loophole. Apparently there wasn't.

"I was a Presidential Scholar, and I only left school midsemester because my father's Alzheimer's got so bad… Yes, I know it looks like I failed those classes, but that's not true. I've got a call in to the dean of students' office to see if we can get that straightened out." The bell on the bookstore door jingled, and she glanced up. Hoyt came in, leading Jess by the hand. He had his go-big-or-go-home expression on his face.

Oh, boy. Not good. And absolutely the last thing she needed right now.

She held up a warning finger, and he nodded. Jess made a beeline for the children's section, but Hoyt leaned his muscled bulk against a wall and crossed his arms in front of his chest, apparently prepared to wait until she got off the phone.

Anna shifted her position so the Bradleys were out of her line of vision and did her best to refocus her attention on her conversation.

"Is there any other kind of financial aid available? Well, may I at least come and talk to you in person? This is really important to me. I need to finish my degree. I see." She sneaked another glance at Hoyt. He was still standing in the same place, and he wasn't even pretending not to eavesdrop on her conversation. "Well, I'll have to find another way, I suppose. Thank you for your time." She ended the call.

"You're going back to college?" Hoyt shot a cautious look in Jess's direction. She'd pulled out three storybooks and had settled herself cross-legged on the floor to examine them. She was paying her father and Anna absolutely no attention, but Hoyt kept his voice down. "What about the store?"

"The store's closing, Hoyt. I have to make other plans." If she could find any that would actually work, that is.

"You know, I never took you for a quitter, Delaney."

Anna froze, her coffee mug halfway to her mouth. "I'm not a quitter."

"Well, closing your dad's bookstore when you've got a solid possibility of saving it sure sounds a lot like quitting to me." He waited a beat or two, watching her. "Anna, we need to talk about what happened at my house."

She'd spent two sleepless nights having imaginary conversations with this man on that very subject, and she'd been brilliant in every one of them. Of course, now that he was standing in front of her, every razor-sharp gibe she'd come up with had gone slap out of her mind.

"Now's not a good time." She shuffled some random papers around. "I'm really busy."

"Yeah. I can see that." Hoyt surveyed the store with one lifted eyebrow. The three of them were its only occupants.

When he glanced back in her direction, his hazel eyes still glimmered with his trademark teasing amusement, but something new was in his expression, as well.

Pity.

Anna's cheeks flushed. Hoyt Bradley, the guy his senior class had affectionately voted "most likely to flunk study hall," felt *sorry* for her.

Her life just kept getting better and better.

"Anna, I owe you an apology. What I said the other night—" he halted, looking uncertain "—I shouldn't have said it," he finished finally. He closed the gap between them and held out his hand. "I hope you'll forgive me."

I shouldn't have said it. Not, *it isn't true.*

Not knowing what else to do, she took his offered hand. His fingers were warm, and his hand was calloused and rough. Most of the men she knew had much softer hands.

This, though, was a working man's hand. A hand that built strong, lasting things.

A hand she should already have let go of. Hoyt was looking at her funny.

She released it quickly and clasped her own hands behind her back, out of the danger zone. Was she ever going to stop embarrassing herself around this guy?

"Don't worry about that. It's fine." Even to her own ears, her voice sounded brittle.

"No, it isn't." Hoyt dropped his big frame onto the spindly antique chair she'd picked up at an estate sale. "I'm sorry I shot off my mouth like that. I know we've got our differences, but back in the day we were friends, me and you." He'd used the incorrect grammar on purpose, to tease her. She saw him waiting for her to make the correction. When she didn't, he sighed and leaned forward, causing the overburdened chair to squeak a protest. "At least we were, until that whole cheating thing came up. You sure didn't have much use for me after that."

He paused as if waiting for her to argue, but she didn't. She only said, "I still don't understand why you did…what you did."

"No. I'm sure you don't." He sounded genuinely regretful, but he didn't elaborate. "But I'm hoping maybe you could see your way to letting bygones be bygones. No offense, but you're kind of going for a gold medal in grudge-holding, Delaney. I'd like to mend our fences, especially since I've got a good bit of skin in this particular game." His eyes strayed over to Jess, who was hunched over the book in her lap. "Besides, this could turn out all right for you, too. I know you care about this store, because I know you cared about your dad. You wouldn't have come home and spent years looking after him, otherwise. And I really do believe I can help you figure out how to stay open. I know you think you're too smart to learn anything from somebody like me—"

Anna flinched. He made her sound like some sort of conceited snot. Was that really how she came across? "That's not true! I don't think any such thing!"

He held her gaze for a minute. She must have passed whatever test he was giving, because he nodded shortly and got to his feet. "Okay. Maybe I misunderstood. In that case, close up the store for the afternoon and come with Jess and me. I want to show you something."

"What?" Anna stood up, too, but only because he was less intimidating that way. A little less. Hoyt Bradley was built like a brick wall.

"Come with me and find out." The mischievous gleam in his eyes had Anna shaking her head before he even finished the sentence. That look was nothing but trouble. The last time she'd seen it, she'd found a half-dissected frog in her backpack.

"Uh-uh."

"Scared?"

"Of you?" *Definitely.* "Don't flatter yourself."

"Prove it."

He held out his hand and wiggled his fingers. The ridiculous man was *daring* her. Anna opened her mouth to say she didn't have to prove anything to him, and, besides, she had work to do. After all, this store wasn't going to close itself.

"All right," she heard herself saying instead. "You're on."

"*This?* This is your big idea? What's *wrong* with you, Hoyt? Are you nuts? There's no way I'm getting in that thing."

Anna had a death grip on the door handle of his truck, and her green eyes were wide. Hoyt coughed. It was either that or laugh, and at this point he figured a laugh would get him swatted.

"That thing is a Cessna 172, and it's a perfectly safe single-engine plane," he stated in his most reasonable tone. "And I'm a legally licensed pilot."

Anna's eyes opened even wider, and she shook her head so hard that her spirally curls swung wildly around the cab. "You seriously expect me to go up in that tin-can contraption with *you* flying it?"

Okay, that stung. He'd worked hard for his license, and he was proud of it. In fact, one of the reasons he'd come up with this idea was to show Anna that he wasn't the blockhead she remembered from their high school days. "I take Jess up all the time. Isn't that right, sweetheart?" From the back seat of his truck, Jess nodded enthusiastically. She loved flying. "You don't think I'd do that if I believed it was dangerous, do you?"

"Sorry. I didn't mean that like it sounded." Anna was looking at the plane through the window, with narrowed eyes. "At least—not entirely. It's just that I don't fly. Ever. Not even on nice big jets with nice big professional pilots in charge. I just *don't*."

Well, all right. That might be a problem.

A loud bang on the side of the truck made them both jump. Hoyt glanced over to see his friend Everett standing beside the pickup, grinning. Hoyt rolled down the window reluctantly.

"What's the matter, Bradley? Can't get the little lady out of the truck?" The older man craned his head around Hoyt to look at Anna. "I don't blame you a bit, honey. You stay right there." He winked. "I sure would if I was you."

"Not funny, Everett," Hoyt muttered under his

breath. Then aloud, he said, "Anna, this is Everett Darden. That plane over there belongs to him."

"Oh!" Anna nodded, and the color came back to her cheeks in a rush. "*He's* the pilot. All that stuff about you flying planes, that was just a joke, right?"

"Oh, Bradley can fly planes all right." Everett's face was solemn, but his eyes were twinkling. "Teaching him to do that was no trouble at all. Teaching him to land 'em, now. That was more problematic. It's how I got most of these gray hairs." He tugged on a lock of the sparse hair that glinted silver in the sunlight.

Anna's mouth dropped open, and Hoyt blew out an exasperated breath.

"Everett, could you rein it in a little? The lady's never flown before."

"Oh." Belated understanding dawned on the older man's face. "I was just joshing, ma'am. I taught this fellow to fly myself, and I'd never have cleared him if he wasn't safe. You won't come to no harm up there with Hoyt. You have my word on it. Now see that plane coming in right now? That's another one of my students. This is his first solo."

Anna focused her attention on the red-and-white Beechcraft Bonanza coming in for a landing, and Hoyt smothered a groan. Just what Anna needed to see right now. An amateur landing a plane by himself for the very first time.

He said a quick prayer for the newbie pilot. *Let him ace this, God. I've got a lot on the line down here.*

Hoyt held his breath as the plane's wings wobbled a little, then steadied. The wheels bumped down gently, and Everett whooped and banged on the side of the truck again.

"Looka there! Perfect landing—or nearabouts, anyway!"

As Everett headed off to congratulate his student, Hoyt studied Anna's face. She was pale, and there was a muscle jumping in her cheek. This whole flying idea was really freaking her out. Maybe he'd better scratch this plan and come up with something else.

"We don't have to do this. I can take you home, and—"

"Can't we take Miss Anna flying, Daddy?" Hoyt glanced in the rearview to see Jess leaning forward against her seat belt, her face pleading. As he watched, his daughter's gaze shifted briefly from him to Anna. "Please?"

His heart locked in place. Was that *please* directed at Anna? Was Jess actually speaking to her?

He wasn't sure, but if so…

If so, that was a really big deal.

What was going to happen when Anna said no? Because judging from the look on her face, there was no way she was going anywhere near that airplane.

Anna's gaze fastened onto his for a second, then she half turned in the front seat to look back at Jess. "Are *you* asking me to go up in that plane, sweetie?" Hoyt held his breath as Jess hesitated, her eyes darting from him to Anna.

"Yes."

It might have been the softest whisper Hoyt had ever heard, but it was definitely an answer. Jess was talking to Anna.

His little girl had just taken another huge step forward.

But the joyful relief that surged up in him was mixed

with fear. Everything he'd prayed for hinged directly on what Anna did next.

He caught her green eyes with his and tried his best to communicate silently. *Please, Delaney. This matters. Please don't say no. Not now.*

He could tell Anna understood him. She instantly went about five shades paler, but she managed a choppy nod. "Well, fine, then. Since *you're* asking me, Jess. Let's do it!"

Hoyt's heart swelled with gratitude—and guilt. "Are you sure?"

"No," she muttered, pushing open the truck door. "I'm not. But I'm doing it anyway."

"What are you up to now?" Anna watched nervously as Hoyt fiddled with various levers and dials inside the cockpit of the plane. "What's wrong? Why haven't we started?"

"Nothing's wrong. I'm going through a preflight checklist. You do it every time you get ready to fly."

"Why? Because something might be wrong?"

"It's a routine safety precaution. We'll get underway in a minute or two." Hoyt glanced over at her and smiled. "Take a few deep breaths and try to relax."

Easy for him to say. He and Jess seemed right at home in this flimsy contraption. She hadn't been far off the mark when she'd described the little plane as a tin can. Anna had been horrified at how light and fragile the door had felt when she'd climbed inside. When she'd pointed it out, Hoyt had laughed.

"You wouldn't want a heavy airplane, would you?"

Well, maybe not. But she'd sure prefer one that didn't

feel like it had come out of some gigantic gumball machine.

Then there were all these complicated dials and gauges spread across the dash in front of her. She couldn't imagine what all these things did, and she absolutely couldn't fathom being in charge of a machine like this. She had trouble navigating the learning curve every time she upgraded her phone.

Yet there was Hoyt Bradley, flipping levers and pushing buttons like some sort of pro. More to the point, here *she* was, sitting beside him, preparing to place her life in the hands of a guy whose main claim to fame was that he was once really good at knocking people down on a football field.

Maybe Hoyt wasn't the one veering into crazy territory here.

But Jess had directly asked her to do this, and Anna hadn't needed Hoyt's unspoken plea to understand how earth-shatteringly important that was. She'd get through this somehow, for Jess's sake.

She had no idea how. But she would.

He turned on a switch, and Anna jumped as the plane's engine sputtered to life. The noise didn't do much to make her feel safer. The thing sounded like a souped-up lawnmower.

"All right! Here we go. Everybody ready?"

Jess clapped, and Anna nodded. It wasn't technically a lie if you didn't say it out loud, right?

Now Hoyt was talking some sort of gibberish into a radio that crackled and spoke gibberish back to him.

Her heart hammering, Anna squeezed her eyes closed and prayed silently. *Please, Lord. Please.* She didn't bother to elaborate. She didn't have to. God knew what she was dealing with.

The plane moved, and her eyes flew open. They were trundling down the pavement, flimsy wings wobbling, apparently headed toward the strip where the other plane had landed.

This was really happening. This glorified cola can was about to be airborne.

By the time Anna realized what was happening, it was already too late. Her breath was coming in short, staccato bursts, and her heart was beating so hard that her chest ached. She couldn't breathe, she couldn't think.

She had to have air.

She had to get *out*.

She began fumbling at the seat belt that held her strapped into the seat.

"Anna, what are you doing? I told you, the seat belt stays on for the whole flight." She heard Hoyt talking, but his voice seemed to come from a distance, muffled by loud gasps that she dimly realized were coming from her own mouth.

"S-stop." It was all she could manage between desperate attempts to suck air into her lungs. Then the gray mist that had fuzzed across her vision darkened, and the whole world went black.

Chapter Four

When she came to, Anna was lying flat on the ground, grass bristling against her back. Somebody had her hand clamped in a death grip, and she whimpered a protest.

The noise only made the painful pressure increase. "I think she's coming around. Anna, hang on, okay? You're going to be fine. Just try to breathe."

The man talking didn't sound like he believed a word he was saying. That had to be Hoyt. He'd never been a good liar. She'd always been able to tell when he hadn't done Mrs. Abercrombie's reading assignments.

Her eyes fluttered open. Sure enough, Hoyt's face swam into wobbly focus. He was kneeling beside her, as white as a sheet, his eyes worried.

As her field of vision widened, she saw that she was surrounded by a circle of men, their faces displaying varying levels of curiosity and concern. Everett held Jess in his arms, and she had her face buried against his plaid shirt.

Everyone else was staring at Anna.

"I'm okay," she managed to croak.

"Of course you are," Hoyt's tone was soothing, but

then he turned his head and barked at the gawking men. "Somebody get her some water!" After a flurry of whispered conversation, two men broke away from the circle and ran off.

The rest of them continued to stare and Anna felt anxiety mounting a second attack on her nervous system.

"Pills," she remembered suddenly. "I have pills in my purse."

Hoyt barked another command, but Anna missed what he said. A shrill, wailing sound drowned out his words.

Sirens. Her glance darted back to Hoyt's face, and she saw relief breaking in his worried eyes.

"Good. The paramedics are here."

Oh, no. "You called an *ambulance*?"

Hoyt seemed taken aback by her dismay. "You passed out, Anna, and you couldn't seem to get a decent breath. So yeah, I called an ambulance. You need to be checked out."

This couldn't be happening. Not here. Not in front of all these people.

Except that it was. She heard doors slamming and running footsteps. The ring of men broke apart to allow two intent-looking men in uniforms to her side.

"Ma'am? Please stay still." They crouched on the ground as Anna attempted to lever herself up on her elbows.

"I'm fine. No, please. You don't need to take my blood pressure. It'll be through the roof. It always is after something like this, but it'll go back down as soon as I get my medicine. Where's that guy with my purse?"

"Ma'am, it's all right. We just need to assess your

situation." The dark-haired paramedic glanced up at the men. "What happened?" He scanned Anna's face, his face a picture of professional concern.

"She couldn't breathe," Hoyt volunteered. "She was gasping for air just before she passed out."

Gasping for air. Anna had a mental picture of herself looking like a landed trout. It wasn't attractive. This was so humiliating.

The medic nodded and then turned his attention back to Anna. "Were you having an asthma attack?"

"No, it's nothing like that."

A balding man in a green T-shirt raced up and threw her shoulder bag in Hoyt's direction. "Here, Bradley, I grabbed her purse out of your truck. Is she all right?"

The second paramedic snagged the bag and unzipped it, rifling through its contents. "What am I looking for, ma'am? An inhaler?" Before she could answer, he unearthed her prescription bottle and scanned its label. Understanding dawned on his face. "Ah. You take these regularly?"

"Not anymore. This is the first time this has happened in months," Anna murmured miserably. She wished the ring of spectators would go away. She really didn't want to have this discussion in front of half of Pine Valley. "I almost threw those pills away."

The paramedic handed her the medicine bottle. "You might want to hang on to them. Panic attacks can be sneaky. You never know what's going to trigger them."

Maybe not. From where she was sitting, Anna could see the plane they'd been in, angled oddly on the runway, its doors gaping open. But sometimes you had a pretty good idea.

She should have seen this coming. Especially after

what she'd found in her father's journal a few weeks ago, she should have—

"A panic attack?" Hoyt echoed. "That's what this was?"

"Yeah, looks like it. You were smart to call 911, though." The second paramedic zipped up his bag. "These things can mimic more serious conditions, and it's always better to be safe than sorry. In fact, I'd like to transport you to the hospital, if that's all right, ma'am. That's standard protocol, and it never hurts to be checked over after something like this."

"No. No, I don't want to go to the hospital." She couldn't afford to pay for that, especially when she knew it wasn't necessary.

"That's totally your choice. I have a waiver you can sign if you're sure."

Josh, the new pilot, skidded up to the group, a bottle of water in his hand. He thrust it at Hoyt. "Here. Is she going to be all right?"

"Yep!" Everett answered, bouncing Jess gently in his arms. "False alarm, thankfully. The lady's going to be just fine. You all can get on back about your business now."

The men started to drift away as Hoyt knelt back down beside Anna and handed her the cold bottle of water. Anna returned the signed waiver to the paramedic and darted a look up at Hoyt's face. He was starting to get some of his color back, but he still looked dazed.

"You're sure she's all right?" he asked the medics.

"As sure as we can be without taking her in for more tests." There was a loud ripping sound as the paramedic unwound the cuff from her arm. "Her blood pressure's up a bit, but that's to be expected. It'll simmer back down. You should go ahead and take one of those pills, ma'am. That'll help." The man turned his attention to Hoyt. "*Bradley*, did they say your name was? Have we met before?"

"Yeah. We have." Pain spasmed across Hoyt's face as he offered the man a handshake. "You answered a call to my home a few years back."

"That's right! Your wife, wasn't it?" The man's eyes flicked to the quivering little girl in Everett's arms, then back at Hoyt. The paramedic nodded once, and for a few seconds the two men shared a long, silent look. Then the other man cleared his throat. "We're all done here. Let me help you up, ma'am."

"I can manage," Anna protested, but this guy was apparently used to ignoring his patients' arguments. He hoisted her to her feet easily.

"Just take it easy the rest of the day. Maybe next time take one of those pills *before* you try getting on an airplane. Okay?"

Anna nodded, but she doubted that would be necessary. From now on, both her feet were staying firmly on the ground.

Her eyes strayed over to Jess. "Is she all right?"

Hoyt turned to check on his trembling daughter and frowned. "Come here, baby." He reclaimed Jess from Everett's arms, and she burrowed her face against her father's neck. "Miss Anna's all right now, but we're not going to get to go up in the airplane today. How about we go get some ice cream at Miss Bailey's store instead?"

No answer.

"Maybe we'll get some of that birthday cake ice

cream you had last time. What would you think about that?" He paused, waiting.

No answer.

"You liked that kind, didn't you?" Nothing. "Or would you rather have strawberry today?"

Anna's heart had started slowing down, but each time Jess didn't answer, it sped back up a notch. She wasn't the only one getting concerned. The color that had ebbed back into Hoyt's cheeks vanished. The agonized expression on his face made her heart ache as the truth sank in.

Jess had gone silent again.

Hoyt parked his truck in front of Pages and glanced in his rearview. Jess was slumped sideways, sound asleep in her booster seat. Hoyt turned his attention to the woman sitting beside him.

Anna's face had lost the gray tinge that had worried him back at the airport, but that was the only positive change he saw. She looked as worn out and defeated as he felt.

The airplane idea was one of the dumbest things he'd ever come up with, that much was for sure. Jess hadn't said one word since the ambulance had shown up, and Delaney might as well have taken the Closed sign out of the bookstore window and stuck it on her forehead. Just like Jess, Anna had shut herself away, and judging by the look on her face, she wasn't coming out any time soon.

Lord, please, help me fix this mess I've made. And if You don't mind, could You spell out how for me? You know I can be pretty thickheaded, and I really can't afford to waste any more time goofing up.

He cleared his throat as she unfastened her seat belt. "I'm really sorry about all that, Anna."

"No." Anna shook her head without any of her usual energy. Her crazy curls barely bounced at all. "I'm the one who's sorry, Hoyt." She glanced into the back seat, where Jess was frowning in her sleep. "Do you think…?" Anna couldn't seem to finish her question.

"I have no idea."

Anna flinched at his tone, and Hoyt sighed. He hadn't meant for his answer to sound harsh. It was just tough to admit that he didn't have a clue what the future held for Jess now. That was a pretty hard thing to face after all the bright hopes he'd clutched onto for the past few days.

"I've ruined everything." Anna seemed to be talking more to herself than to him, but he answered her anyway.

"None of this is your fault. This is all on me." That was true, but admitting it sure didn't make him feel any better. "It was plain as day that you were terrified to get on that plane. You'd never have done it if you hadn't been trying to help Jess. I shouldn't have *let* you do it."

Some spunk sparkled back into Anna's expression. "Last time I checked, I don't take orders from you, Bradley. Anyway, I should've seen that panic attack coming a mile away. I've struggled with anxiety off and on ever since my mom died, but I haven't had an attack in months, even with the stress I've been dealing with. I'd thought maybe I was past that. Obviously not." She sent another worried glance into the back seat. "I'll be praying for Jess. For both of you."

When Anna opened the truck door and stepped out, Hoyt suddenly came to. He couldn't just dump this woman at the curb, not after everything he'd put her through this afternoon. "Wait a second. I'll walk with you." But when he opened his own door, she leaned back into the cab, shaking her head.

"No, I can manage from here. But I'd really appreciate it if you'd let me know if Jess—" Anna stopped short and then tried again "—how Jess does. Okay?"

"Sure." He felt rude just sitting in the truck, but he'd probably pushed Anna Delaney far enough for one day. He watched her walk to the door of her bookstore, moving as if she was bone weary.

She probably was. Stress was a killer. Marylee's illness had been the most exhausting time of his life, and weathering Jess's silence hadn't been any picnic, either. He'd been tired and worried for so long he'd forgotten what it felt like to live any other way.

Until recently. These last few days had been different. Part of it was the relief of finally seeing some progress and having something he could actually do to help Jess move forward.

But he'd also kind of liked trading barbs with Anna Delaney again, like they had back in high school. It had almost felt like he'd hit some cosmic reset button on his life and gone back to a time before everything went sideways on him.

He'd felt really—*awake*, for the first time in a long, long time. But after the mess he'd made today, all that was over with, and he had nobody to blame for it but himself.

He was pulling away from the curb when his mind replayed something Anna had said. *Ever since my mom died.*

Whoa.

Stunned, Hoyt jolted the truck back into Park so hard he double-checked to make sure he hadn't woken Jess up. She was still sleeping, so he focused on the half-forgotten memory tickling around the edges of his mind.

There'd been some story about Anna's mother's death, hadn't there? Something...*bad.* What was it?

Leaving the truck idling, he yanked his phone out of his shirt pocket and thumbed up a search engine. It took him a while, but he finally found it.

And immediately wished he hadn't. He read the headline with horror.

Local Art Teacher Perishes in Plane Crash.

Oh, wow.

He sat there for a few seconds, kicking himself for being so stupid and—what was that other word Marylee had thrown around sometimes when he'd said or done some really boneheaded thing?

Insensitive.

That, he'd learned, was a female word for "lower than dirt." During his short marriage, he must've discovered at least a hundred ways to get himself called insensitive. Fortunately, the remedy for it was always the same: a big apology, a double handful of the prettiest flowers he could find and a long kiss.

He'd definitely done some dumb stuff in his time, but he couldn't remember ever messing up quite this bad before. And he sure couldn't fall back on his standby apology tactics. Imagine him...kissing Anna Delaney.

How crazy would *that* be?

A few minutes later, he realized he was still sitting in his truck, staring blankly at his dusty dashboard.

He blinked and shook his head. He must've zoned out there for a minute.

Anyway, he didn't have time to sit here feeling guilty. He'd have to figure out how to apologize to Anna later. Right now he had even bigger problems to deal with. He'd get Jess back to the house and see if Dr. Mills could work in a quick phone consultation. Maybe together they could figure out some kind of damage control that would get Jess talking again.

He just hoped that whatever they came up with didn't hinge on asking Anna Delaney for any more favors.

Chapter Five

"So? What do you think I should do?" Relieved he was finally done stumbling through his retelling of the mess he'd made, Hoyt waited for Jacob Stone's answer.

He didn't have to wait long.

"I think you should ask Anna to talk to Jess and explain what happened." The pastor of Pine Valley Community Church leaned back in his squawking office chair as Hoyt groaned. "What?"

Two days had passed since the airplane incident, and Jess still hadn't spoken a word. Hoyt hadn't been able to get in touch with Dr. Mills, and the therapist's voice message said her inbox was too full for additional messages. He knew she would call when she could, but he also had a gut feeling that he needed to act fast if he was going to get Jess talking again.

He'd come to Jacob out of a desperate need to do *something.* The local minister was pretty good at figuring out dicey situations, and Hoyt had hoped Jacob might have a suggestion.

A *helpful* suggestion. Not one that had disaster written all over it.

Jacob frowned as he considered Hoyt's expression. "Do you really want to hear my opinion on this? Because selective mutism is pretty far outside my wheelhouse."

"You know everybody involved, and I trust you. So, yeah. I want to hear your take on this. I'm just not sure dragging Anna back into this is the best idea."

Jacob's lips twitched. "I can see why. That plane screwup of yours was epic."

Stone never pulled any punches. Normally that was something Hoyt appreciated. Right now he wasn't so sure. "I apologized, but I seriously doubt Anna's going to be willing to do any more favors for me."

"Maybe not, but the only way to find out is to ask her. I'm a big believer in being direct."

Hoyt knew that better than most. Back in the dark days after Marylee's death, when Hoyt had started drinking to dull his pain, the preacher had squared off with him and said the hard things that had needed saying.

Hoyt didn't like to think what could have happened to him—or to Jess—if it hadn't been for the unflinching honesty of the man sitting across this desk.

"I could be wrong, of course," the pastor continued. "But in my experience kids respond well to honesty. If I were you, I'd ask Anna to tell Jess exactly why she panicked in the airplane."

"I just don't see what good that could do at this point. Anna's mom died in a plane crash, remember, and that's probably the last thing Jess needs to hear about right now. What if bringing it back up just freaks them both out all over again?"

"First of all, don't start thinking *what if.* Those two

words almost never lead you down any path you'd want to be on. And second, I don't know what the result will be, and neither do you. No matter how hard you try, Hoyt, some things, some important things, are always going to fall outside of your control. That's where faith comes in."

"Maybe you're right. It just sounds risky to me."

"Everything worthwhile involves some risk." Jacob's eyes cut to a photograph on his desk that showed his pretty wife, Natalie, holding his adopted son, Ethan, in her arms. A little smile tipped up his lips, and he spoke again without looking away from the picture. "God usually shines His light only on the next step we're supposed to take. He wants us to trust Him for the rest of it." Jacob stood and held out his hand. "But believe me, He always comes through. And when He does, it's amazing."

"All right." Hoyt shook the minister's hand. "You win. I'll ask Anna to talk to Jess. But you'd better toss up a few extra prayers because Delaney wasn't any big fan of mine *before* I scared her out of her wits in that airplane."

"You never know." Jacob grinned. "Anna might surprise you."

"She generally does."

At seven forty-five the next morning, Hoyt pulled his truck up in front of the bookstore and glanced in the rearview mirror. Jess blinked curiously at him from her booster seat.

"Remember what I told you, sweetheart? We're going to stop in and see Miss Anna before going to day care." An instant smile lit up Jess's freckled face.

Not too long ago, those smiles had been the highlights of his days, but they weren't enough anymore. He desperately needed to hear the sweet piping sound of his daughter's voice again.

Please, Lord, let this work.

He hoped Jacob was right about all this. He wished he could've checked in with Dr. Mills before going ahead with the stunt the preacher had proposed, but she hadn't responded to his text. He suspected that meant her mother's condition had worsened, and he didn't feel comfortable pestering the therapist while she was coping with a family crisis.

Anna, on the other hand, had answered on the first ring about half an hour ago. He'd waited that long to call, even though it meant going in late to the job site on a busy day. He hadn't waited long enough, apparently. Anna had sounded sleepy.

And confused. "You want me to do *what*?"

Hoyt tried explaining again, although he didn't think he'd done a better job of it the second time. He trusted Jacob Stone more than any other man alive, but this still seemed like a low-down thing to ask somebody to do.

I'm asking you to talk about your personal pain—about the thing that left such a big scar on your life that you've had to take pills to get over it—just on the slim hope that it'll help my little girl start talking again. You don't mind, do you?

If somebody had asked him to do something like that after Marylee's death, he'd probably have slugged them.

Jacob Stone thought this was a good idea, but the minister never balked at asking people for favors—or at doing them. He seemed to feel that was all part of being a practicing Christian. But Hoyt didn't much like approaching anybody with his hand out. And somebody like Anna? Somebody who right now probably felt like she owed him a swift kick rather than a favor?

He definitely didn't like asking her.

But for Jess's sake he had. And after a short hesitation, Anna had agreed.

"If you and Pastor Stone think it would help, of course I'll talk to Jess. Or I'll try. I've never...talked much about that before to anybody. What if I make things worse?"

What if. Jacob's warning echoed in Hoyt's memory.

"Take a shot, Anna. That's all I'm asking."

"All right. Come on in before the store opens. Maybe in half an hour? Would that work?"

He'd told her, sure. That'd work. Of course, if she'd told him to show up in the middle of the night wearing a tuxedo and scuba flippers, he'd have made that work, too.

So here he was.

Movement inside the store caught his attention. Anna was unlatching the bookstore's door. She looked up, and their eyes met. For a second, she studied him, chewing on her bottom lip. Then her gaze slid away from his toward the rear seat of his king cab, where Jess always rode. Anna tightened her lips, looked back at him and gave him a short nod.

He recognized that look. He'd felt it on his own face more times than he could count.

Anna was cowboying up. She was steeling herself to go through with this, no matter how uncomfortable it made her, because he'd told her it might help Jess.

That was Anna. She never backed down from doing what she thought was right, no matter how tough it was.

You might not always know where you stood with Anna Delaney, but you sure always knew where *she* stood.

Smack-dab in the middle of the straight and narrow. Every single time.

Hoyt's mind flitted back to the hopeful remark Jacob Stone had tossed off in his church office. *She might surprise you.*

Nope, Hoyt realized. As a matter of fact, Anna hadn't surprised him at all.

As Anna opened the door of the bookstore, the familiar smells of an early summer morning wafted in. There was a whiff of damp asphalt, the musty odor of the old canvas awnings shading her share of sidewalk and the comforting tease of cinnamon from the church coffee shop across the square.

Everything was perfectly ordinary, Anna reassured herself. Everything was fine.

She could totally do this. In fact, if there was any hope that talking about her panic attack would help Jess, she *had* to do this.

She pasted a wobbly smile on her face as Hoyt and Jess approached. Jess looked as adorable as always. Her blond ponytail bobbed, and her sneakers lit up with some sort of built-in sparkles as she skipped along the sidewalk, her little fingers twined trustingly around her dad's hand.

Anna had a sudden image of broad-shouldered Hoyt picking out tiny pink shoes, paying extra for the ones that lit up in order to tease a smile from his grieving daughter. A confusing flood of emotions washed through her.

Hoyt could annoy the paint right off a wall, but there

was no getting around it—the man definitely had his good points.

Anna snapped the lid on her warm, fuzzy feelings as fast as she could and shoved them away. She didn't need any of those weird, Hoyt-inspired flutters. Not right now. She already had more than enough to cope with. Still, she couldn't help glancing up into his face as he neared her, and what she saw only made her jangled nerves swirl around more.

He looked exhausted. Judging by the dark smudges under his eyes and those tense grooves around his mouth, he hadn't slept much since she'd last seen him. Jess going silent again was killing him. He caught her looking and offered her a tired, hopeful smile. Immediately Anna's already-hammering heartbeat accelerated into a gear she hadn't known existed.

Even exhausted, this man's smile packed a serious punch.

Anna drew in one of those good, slow breaths her psychology professor used to encourage. One thing was for sure. She was *not* going to have another panic attack in front of Jess. She'd already taken one of her pills as a precaution, and, given the way her pulse was skittering around right now, it was a good thing she had. She doubted she could make this situation any better, but she was determined not to make it any worse.

"Good morning!" The greeting echoed in the empty store, too loud and too cheery. Anna didn't need the startled look Jess threw at her to know that she was already blowing this.

The little girl started toward her favorite bookshelf, then halted and glanced at Anna. Her father must have explained that they weren't here for an ordinary book-browsing expedition. Anna swallowed hard and smiled.

"Jess, there's something I wanted to show you up in my apartment. Want to come see?"

Jess nodded, curiosity sparkling in her blue eyes. So far, so good. As Anna led the way over to the worn wooden steps that led to her loft, she realized that Hoyt was following them.

Wait a minute. Hoyt was coming, too? She definitely hadn't counted on that.

She'd rehearsed her fumbling little talk half a dozen times since Hoyt's unexpected phone call, but never once had it occurred to her that he'd be listening in. What she planned to talk about was—personal.

It was hard enough to share it with Jess, but talking about it with Hoyt in the room, *looking* at her the whole time? She'd never be able to pull that off. She tripped over the top riser of the steps, and Hoyt reached out a quick arm to catch her elbow.

"Steady, there." His voice was casual and so was his touch, but Anna's stupid flutters shot into the stratosphere anyway.

Okay, it was official. She was toast.

Hoyt scanned the loft area with interest, apparently oblivious to her uneasiness. "I've never been upstairs in one of these store buildings before. I guess back in the day a lot of the store owners lived above their businesses. Pretty convenient, really."

"My apartment's on the left. These rooms on the right are just storage." She pulled the door closest to her shut, but it immediately popped back open again. "This one never shuts well."

"You probably just need a new doorknob. Let me see."

"That's okay. Don't worry about it."

Too late. Hoyt had grabbed the knob and pushed the door fully open. Or as far open as it would go. He whistled through his teeth. "You've got a lot of stuff crammed in here, Anna."

Well, this was embarrassing. She'd spent the whole last half hour tidying up her apartment while talking out loud to herself, practicing what she was going to say. And now Hoyt had zeroed in on the one area in the whole building that she was most ashamed of.

"I know. It's stuff from the old house. My dad's book collection mostly. The house sold fast, and I had to clean it out in a hurry. I haven't had the time to finish going through it."

Or the heart. Not since she'd stumbled across her father's journal.

After reading that, she'd stopped going through her father's belongings. She really couldn't handle any more emotional land mines right now.

She'd made a feeble attempt to organize all the junk. She'd even bought some cheap shelves and put them together all by herself. She hadn't done a very good job; they swayed a lot when you touched them. But at least they helped get some of the stuff off the floor until she felt capable of coping with it.

She reached past him and pulled the door firmly closed. Of course it didn't catch and popped right back open, but Hoyt took the hint and stepped back into the hallway.

As Anna opened the door to her small living area, her embarrassment lingered. Hoyt's home had been so airy and well planned and attractive. Hers was exactly the opposite, cramped and makeshift, with a generous side of shabby. On a good day, she told herself the place had the feel of a trendy bohemian loft, with its exposed wooden rafters, scarred floorboards, and mix-and-match furniture in various hues of blue and green.

On a bad day, she fixated on the impossibly stained fixtures in the tiny bathroom, the musty smell she couldn't seem to get rid of and the fact that every stick of furniture in the place was older than she was.

She'd moved into the apartment after her father's death, when she'd been forced to sell their cozy suburban brick home to settle outstanding medical bills. At the time, she'd just been thankful to have someplace to go. The financial situation she'd been left with had been pretty scary. But now she felt uncomfortably aware that, while a place like this would be perfectly fine for a young undergrad, for a woman her age and with her level of education, it was a little…pathetic.

Hoyt glanced around, his hazel eyes sharp with interest. He flicked the wobbly light switch off and on and frowned. "Has this building ever been rewired?"

"I have no idea. Probably not."

Hoyt stooped to inspect an outlet. His frown darkened. "You might want to think about having it done. These fixtures are really outdated. Mind if I poke around a little while you and Jess talk?"

"Go ahead." If Hoyt wanted to do an impromptu building inspection, at least that would give her some privacy while she talked to Jess. He was wasting his time finding things that needed fixing, though. She could barely manage to pay her electrical bill these days; there was no way she could afford to have the place rewired.

Hoyt disappeared into the kitchen, and Anna sat on the couch, patting the worn cushion beside her invitingly. “Come sit by me, Jess.”

Jess obediently sat, giggling as the cushion dipped deeply under her slight weight. Anna smiled.

“This couch is pretty old. But you know what? I still like to take naps on it. I’ve had it forever, and I really don’t mind it being saggy. It almost feels like it’s hugging me when I lie down.”

Jess’s smile broadened. She bounced silently on the couch, making the spent springs squeak. Anna heard a door creak as Hoyt moved from the kitchen into the bathroom. She’d better hurry up. Reaching behind a green throw pillow, she produced a very worn, very limp brown-and-white stuffed dog.

When she’d quickly prayed for help with this talk, this toy was the only thing that had come to mind. At first she’d hesitated, but then she’d gone to the box in her closet and taken him out.

God specialized in bringing beauty from ashes, didn’t He? She’d see what He could do with this.

She handed the toy to Jess. “This is Chester. I’ve had him since I was a little girl.”

Jess examined the dilapidated puppy carefully and glanced back up at Anna, one eyebrow cocked.

What’s this about? the little girl seemed to be asking.

This was even harder than she’d thought. *Please, God, help me here. I have no idea how to talk about this.*

“You know how your mom passed away when you were really little? Well, when I was eight, my mom died in a plane crash.” There. It was out. Anna braced herself. Jess's expression didn't change much. She just looked down and started toying with one of Chester's floppy ears. "That's why I got so scared in the airplane the other day, even though your dad is a *really* safe pilot. Sometimes when I think about my mom or about airplanes, my feelings can get a little too big for me to handle. I'm really sorry if I frightened you."

One almost imperceptible shoulder shrug was Jess's only response.

"Maybe I should have taken Chester with me. He's always been really good at helping me handle my feelings."

Jess glanced between Chester and Anna, and her eyebrow cocked up again.

Anna kept her smile in place, trying not to show how nervous she was about where this conversation was headed. "I found Chester on my pillow the morning my mother left on her trip. I'd been begging for a puppy, but we couldn't have one because my father was allergic. My dad said she'd left him to keep me company while she was gone. After my mom died, of course, I had a lot of big feelings to deal with. And my dad…well, he loved me so much. But the problem was, he was dealing with his own big feelings. When I tried to talk to him about how I missed my mom, it upset him. Once it even made him cry. So I stopped talking to him about it, but then I started having nightmares. Sometimes," Anna leaned close and whispered, "I even wet the bed."

Jess's eyes widened comically at that admission, and Anna smiled. "Yeah, I know. I was way too old for that kind of thing. But now and then, when our feelings are too big for us, things like that happen. Fortunately I found out something about Chester." Anna reached out and stroked the dog's misshapen head with a gentle finger. "He has a superpower. He's a *really* great listener. He never cried or worried or got scared himself, but he always seemed to understand when I did. He was just the *best* buddy to have whenever my feelings got a little too much for me to handle. And that's why I'm giving him to you."

"You don't have to do that, Anna."

The deep voice startled Anna so much that she jumped, making the worn-out springs of her old sofa jiggle. Her cheeks flushed hot. How long had Hoyt been leaning against the kitchen doorframe? How much had he heard?

Before she could answer him, Jess leaped up from the couch, with Chester clutched tightly in her arms.

"Please let me have Chester, Daddy!" Jess made her plea as naturally as any ordinary five-year-old. She hugged the floppy dog against her T-shirt. "I have big feelings, too, just like Miss Anna did. I *need* him."

As Hoyt stared at his daughter, relief and joy broke over his face, smoothing out all those tight, weary lines. But when he spoke, his voice only shook a little.

"Okay then, baby. If Miss Anna really doesn't mind."

"I've actually been considering adopting a real live dog, so I don't mind a bit." She didn't. The truth was, she'd been tempted to put her once-beloved little toy in the trash, given what she'd read in that journal.

She was glad she hadn't given in to that impulse. God really had brought beauty from ashes, just like the Bible said.

Thank You, Lord.

Jess bounced up and down, hugging the scruffy toy. "Thanks, Daddy!" The little girl turned her blue eyes on Anna's face. "I'll take extra good care of him, I *promise*!"

Anna nodded. She was having some trouble squeezing words past the peach-sized lump in her throat. "I know," she managed finally. "Oh, I know you will, sweetie. You'll take wonderful care of him."

When Jess turned her attention back to Chester, Anna made the mistake of glancing up at Hoyt. He was looking straight at her now, with an expression so direct and so intense that her heartbeat stammered in response to it.

Thank you, he mouthed.

Her face went hot, then cold, and tears pricked at the back of her eyes. *You're so very welcome. It was the least I could do.* That was what she should have told him, or something along those lines. But for some reason, looking into his shining hazel eyes, Anna couldn't say a word.

All she could do was smile.

Chapter Six

The following morning, Hoyt stood in front of Pages, kicking the cracked curbing with the toe of his work boot. He glanced at his watch for the third time in five minutes. He'd have to get to the job site soon. Mitch needed him to do a walk-through before the county inspector showed up this afternoon.

Hoyt craned his neck to peer in through the window. Anna was still talking to Trish.

He'd wait out here a little longer. He didn't have time to waste passing pleasantries with Trisha Saunders this morning. He had more important things on his agenda.

He'd dropped Jess off at day care a little while ago. She'd chattered to him the whole way, clutching that worn-out stuffed puppy Anna had given her.

She'd clammed up the minute they'd arrived at the center just like always, but he was focusing on his blessings today. At least Jess had regained the ground she'd lost, and there was every reason to hope she'd keep moving forward. He had Anna to thank for that.

It was funny, what you didn't know about people. He'd known Anna's mother was dead, but he'd never stopped to think about what that must have meant to a girl growing up. All those hours they'd spent together with her coaxing him page by page through some boring book, he'd never given much thought to what her personal life was like.

Pretty selfish of him. Then again, he'd had so much trouble on his own plate back then that he hadn't had much time to pay attention to other people's problems.

He looked at his watch again. He really needed to get to work. He leaned over to look through the window again, hoping to see some sort of sign that Anna and Trish's conversation was coming to a close.

He saw no hint of that, but what he *did* see had him abandoning the curb and striding into the bookstore.

"What's wrong?" It was more of a demand than a question, and both women jumped.

"Hoyt Bradley!" Trish pressed one hand against her heart and shot him an irritated look. "You nearly scared the life out of me, bursting in here like that!"

Hoyt ignored her. "Anna? Are you all right?"

"I'm fine."

"Of course she is!" For a second Trish's annoyance flashed plainly, then she shot another wary look in Hoyt's direction. The florist reached out and patted Anna's arm. "Anna and I were just settling up some things, that's all. We women aren't like you hard-hearted men, Hoyt. When we have to close up a business, it feels like we're giving up one of our children." Trish's hand strayed to her own round belly, and she offered him a gentle smile. "Well, not *quite* like that, of course. But close. Especially when you don't have any real family to focus on. Isn't that right, Anna?"

Anna quietly moved her arm out of patting range.

"Did you need something, Hoyt? Trisha was just leaving."

Trisha's expression shifted from smug back to irked. "I suppose I do need to get back to the shop. I have weddings booked every weekend from now through November. That's why I can't keep this expansion on the back burner any longer. I've simply got to have more space." Trish tapped a paper on the checkout counter with one brightly painted nail. "You have my offer, Anna, and like I said, it's take it or leave it. Let me know."

Trish shot Anna one last hard glance that Hoyt didn't much like and then made a point of brushing against him as she went out the door, even though there was plenty of space. Trish always had been a flirt, and her marriage hadn't changed that as much as it should have.

But he wasn't worried about Trisha's morals right now. "Let me see that." Before Anna could argue, he pulled the paper toward him and skimmed it.

He was scowling before he made it halfway down the page. The offer was a few digits short of outright robbery. "You're crazy if you agree to this price. She's ripping you off."

"It's not as much as I'd hoped to get, that's for sure. But given my circumstances, and the condition of the building, I'm not sure I have much choice." The defeat in Anna's voice made him look up at her. He didn't like the way that expression changed her face, not one bit.

He also didn't like what her remark about the building reminded him of. He hesitated, hating to pile on any more trouble when she was already having such a tough morning. But some things really couldn't wait.

"This building does need some work. That wiring in your apartment was installed back before people had all the electrical appliances we use now. It's not built to handle the load you've got on it. Plus, it's just plain worn out. Poking around up there, I saw exposed wiring and some jacklegged repairs that aren't even close to being up to code. I meant to talk with you about that yesterday, but then—"

"Then Jess talked." The worried creases between Anna's brows smoothed a little. "How's she doing this morning?"

"Really good." He forgot about Anna's problems for a second or two as he recounted their chattery trip into town. "That's why I came in today, to thank you. That talk and that stuffed dog, Charlie—"

"Chester."

"Right. Chester. He really did the trick. I feel bad about you having to give him up, though."

"Don't." She spoke so sharply that it took him back for a second. But then she smiled. "Honestly, I was glad to do it."

There was no mistaking the sincerity in her voice. But still. "Well, I owe you big for that one, Anna, and I won't forget it." He wouldn't. He'd find some way to pay her back. In fact, he already had one idea. It was a little crazy, and he might not be able to pull it off. But he was looking into it.

"You don't owe me a thing, Hoyt. It was my freak-out in that airplane that set Jess back in the first place." She tilted her head, considering him. "You know, I'm still trying to wrap my mind around the fact that you're a pilot. That's a really big accomplishment. Congratulations."

She was using the compliment as a subject changer. More proof that Anna Delaney was one smart woman because it worked like a charm. Funny how a few simple words could warm a man's insides up like a cup of hot coffee on a chilly day.

"Thanks."

"How did you get interested in flying?"

He'd been asked that before, lots of times. He had a stock answer, an answer that told enough of the truth to be believable but not enough to raise any eyebrows.

He started to give it, and then he remembered Anna sitting on the couch with his daughter, her fingers clenched together so tightly that her knuckles were paper white, talking about the toughest time in her life as honestly as she could.

He owed this woman the truth.

"I took it up after Marylee died because I'd started drinking."

The curiosity in Anna's eyes flashed into shock and then gentled into a cautious sympathy. "Did it help?"

"Yeah, but not for the reason I thought it would. I was just...lost without Marylee. We got together so young we pretty much grew up together. I honestly didn't know where I stopped and she started." He had to stop and clear his throat. "When she was sick... Well, it was tough. Then when she was gone and Jess quit talking, the pain got to be so much that I started hitting the bottle. Dumbest thing I could have done, I know."

"Pain like that could make anybody do dumb things, Hoyt." Anna's voice was gentle.

"You sound like the preacher. Stone was the one who put me onto the idea of flying. It was one hobby I definitely couldn't do if I was drinking. Everett made me blow in a tube before every lesson to make sure. That's why I started. But I kept on because..." He paused and then forged ahead. "Maybe it sounds bad, but everything around this town made me think of Marylee, and I was so sick of hurting all the time. Flying was something new, something she'd never been a part of. It's hard to explain, but it gave me some of the only relief I got, back then."

"No, I understand. When my father died—" She stopped and flushed. "I'm sorry. I know losing a parent isn't the same as losing a wife."

He shook his head. "Loss is loss, Anna. And grieving somebody you loved isn't ever anything you should apologize for."

A little humor sparkled back into her eyes. "Now who's sounding like Pastor Stone?"

Hoyt grinned. Well, that was new. Nobody'd ever accused him of sounding like a preacher before. "I guess the man rubs off on you. And I'll admit he does have good ideas. The flying helped me even more than I thought it would. When I saw Pine Valley spread out underneath the wings of that plane, suddenly things just made more *sense*. Know what I mean?"

Her green eyes were focused very intently on his now, and she shook her head slowly. "No, I don't think I do."

Hoyt struggled to figure out some way to explain it. "The surprising thing when you're up in the air is how..." he searched for the right word "...*connected* everything seems. It's seeing everything at the same time, I guess. And maybe seeing some things that you wouldn't ordinarily see at all. Like I noticed Pete Garwood was out working in his yard in the middle of a workday, and I recalled hearing that the company he worked for was laying folks off right and left. He owed me money, Garwood did, for an addition I'd put on his house some months back, and I was getting pretty aggravated with him until I put two and two together." He was making a mess of this explanation, but he couldn't see any way to do better, so he just kept going. "Flying helped me understand people around here better. It gave me more..." He trailed off again, searching for the right word.

"Perspective." Anna supplied it quietly.

"Right." He paused, trying to figure out how to say what he wanted to say next. "That's partly why I wanted to take you flying. Because I thought maybe that's what it'll take to turn this bookstore around. Some perspective on what the folks around here are really like, you know? What they're interested in."

Anna sighed. "Maybe. I've done a lot of research on the best ways to market books, and of course, I know the things my dad used to do to drum up business. I really wanted to do one of those author chats he used to host here. I even have a lead on a bestselling author who's willing to come. That would be a huge boost. But things like that cost money, and I just don't have it. You know what they say. It takes money to make money."

She had a point there. Hoyt hesitated. He dimly recalled those author chats—mainly because Principal Delaney was always badgering him to attend one. He never had, and the way he remembered it, not that many other people had, either. But maybe he was wrong. Anyway, there was no doubt that Anna knew a lot more about books than he did. If she thought one of those author chat things was going to be the key to turning this bookstore around, maybe she was right.

"How much would something like that run you?"

Anna thought for a minute and then named a figure. Hoyt reached into his back pocket and pulled out his checkbook.

"What are you doing?"

"Investing." He scribbled out the check and laid it on the counter.

Anna stared at it in horror. "I can't let you do that!"

"You can. Or you can sell out to Trisha for next to nothing." He tapped Trisha's offer with one finger. "Your call, but I have to tell you, I'd sure hate to see you sell your dad's dream for a bogus amount like this. It doesn't seem right."

Judging by the look on Anna's face, he'd gone at this from the best possible angle. She studied the check for a few silent seconds. Then she shook her head.

"I can't, though. You'd probably just be wasting that money, no matter what I try at this point."

"That's a risk I'm willing to take. I'm serious, Anna. Jess is talking because of you and this store. I don't pretend to understand why, but she is. I have a stake in what happens to this place, too."

Anna hesitated while he watched hope and worry battling it out in her eyes. Hope won out. "All right. I'll accept the check on two conditions. First, on the understanding that I'll pay it back with interest just as soon as I can."

"Not necessary, but if you want to do that, fine. What's the second condition?"

Anna pulled a hardback book off a nearby display and shoved it in his direction. "That you buy this, and come to the author chat. If you're sponsoring the event, you should at least attend."

Whoa.

He spun the book around with the tip of his finger and read the title. *The Seventh Scaffold* by somebody named James Coulter. There wasn't even a scaffold on the cover, just a cracked vase with a flower lying beside it. "I'll buy it, sure. Do I have to read it?"

"Hoyt."

"Ring it up, then."

He couldn't quite keep the gloom out of his voice, and Anna shook her head. "You know, you might actually enjoy this book, Hoyt."

"I guess anything's possible." Hoyt dug for his wallet as the bells on the cash register rang.

He was being polite. The chances of him liking any book sporting a flower on its cover were slim to none.

On the other hand, he sure was enjoying seeing that spunk sparkling in Anna Delaney's eyes again.

A couple of weeks later, Anna kept her determined smile plastered on her face and adjusted the sign that read Author Chat with James Coulter, which she'd positioned next to the stack of his books.

This event had to go well. She literally couldn't afford for anything to go wrong. The problem was, when a former college classmate became a bestselling author, he didn't necessarily stop being a total pain in the neck.

James had arrived almost an hour early tonight, wanting to make sure that his lengthy list of pre-event demands had been met. Ignoring her assurances, he'd insisted on ticking through the list item by item. Sparkling water, a particular style of pen and an array of organic, gluten-free snacks that she'd had to ask boutique grocer Bailey Quinn to special-order.

That was fine. She had all that covered, plus she'd

paid him an only slightly reduced honorarium for coming, so he should have been happy.

He wasn't.

"I'm sorry, Anna, but this really seems like a waste of my time. How many of my books could you possibly hope to sell in a one-horse town like this?"

"Oh, I think you might be surprised."

Technically she was telling the truth. Even *she* was surprised by how few of his books she'd managed to sell out of the modest fifty she'd ordered. The number was even more depressing when you considered that one had been to herself and another was the one she'd strong-armed Hoyt into buying.

At least some people had shown up. She'd squeezed twenty-five chairs into the main area of the cramped store, and half of them were filled already. This was the most people she'd ever had in the store at one time, and hopefully at least some of them would buy a copy of Coulter's book before they left.

One person was conspicuously absent, though. Hoyt Bradley was nowhere to be seen.

Coulter made an impatient noise and glanced at his flashy watch. "I have to drive back to Atlanta to catch a flight to Tampa first thing in the morning, so I can't run late tonight."

"Of course. It's time to get started anyway." As she spoke she saw Hoyt edging into the bookstore. *Finally!* "But first there's somebody I'd like you to meet." Ignoring the writer's annoyed huff of breath, she took him by one suede elbow patch and steered him in Hoyt's direction.

Coulter balked when they were about five feet away from Hoyt. Anna didn't blame Coulter for keeping a wary distance. Next to the narrow-shouldered author, Hoyt looked even more massive than usual. He was wearing a plain white button-up shirt with no tie, and his biceps had the short sleeves filled to full capacity.

"Mr. Coulter, this is Hoyt Bradley. He's the businessman who sponsored this event."

"Oh." Relief relaxed the writer's face as he extended his hand. "A philanthropist. Nice to make your acquaintance."

Hoyt uncrossed his arms long enough to grip the man's hand. Coulter winced, and Anna shot Hoyt a warning look. He met her gaze blandly. "Sure thing."

"I'll look forward to your input during the roundtable. I always enjoy hearing from my male readers. So often these events are totally dominated by women." Coulter skimmed the milling crowd with a sigh, flexing his injured hand. "I'll be especially interested in hearing a masculine perspective on Blaine's inner conflict."

Hoyt smiled without answering. Anna's eyes narrowed. She'd seen that particular smile dozens of times back in high school. She knew exactly what it meant.

He didn't have the foggiest idea what the author was talking about. Hoyt hadn't read the book. She'd better get Coulter away before he figured that out for himself.

"Look at the time! We should get started." She put a hand on Coulter's arm and tugged him toward the front of the room. "I'll talk to you later, Hoyt."

It was as much a threat as a promise, but Hoyt only looked amused. Anna got Coulter settled behind an old podium she'd dragged out from the back room and repainted a glossy brown. It was still slightly sticky, and she noticed her guest wrinkling his nose as he touched it.

Great. Something else for him to complain about.

Please, Lord, she prayed as she encouraged people to take their seats. *You know how badly I need this to go well. Help me make this a success.* With a bright smile, she introduced James Coulter, an award-winning, bestselling author, to the murmuring group, sat herself down and hoped for the best.

Forty-five long minutes later, Anna's polite smile had grown painfully stiff. She was bored out of her mind, and judging by the restless shiftings behind her, she wasn't the only one. Not only was Coulter horribly dull as a speaker, but he oozed a pompous arrogance that was making her toes curl.

Still, she reassured herself, he was a well-known name, and his book had been positively reviewed. Lots of gifted people weren't good public speakers, and maybe he'd do better during the interactive session of the evening.

She sure hoped so.

"Thank you so much, Mr. Coulter, for that wonderful explanation of scaffolding symbolism." She was fairly sure that was what he'd been droning on about. "Now we're going to have a brief intermission before moving on to the most exciting part of our evening. In fifteen minutes, you'll have the opportunity to participate in a roundtable discussion with this famous author. In the meantime, you can enjoy some refreshments, chat with Mr. Coulter and get him to sign his book. Copies are located on the table by the door, if you haven't already purchased one."

She suppressed a little shudder of dismay when the audience moved in the direction of the refreshments instead of the optimistic stacks of books on Coulter's signing table. She'd better shoo some people in Coulter's direction.

She'd start with Bailey Quinn, one of the few who'd actually bought a copy of the book ahead of time. The grocery store owner was nibbling on an organic baby carrot when Anna approached.

Anna reached for the plate holding the Coulter-approved snacks that she'd prepared earlier. "Bailey, would you please take this over to James? He's bound to have questions about the food, and you'll probably be the best one to answer, since I bought most of it from you."

"Sure." Bailey didn't look any too enthusiastic, but she set down her own plate and accepted the one Anna handed her.

"Have you seen Hoyt?"

"Yeah. He sneaked out about halfway through. I noticed because I was kind of wishing I could go with him." Bailey shot Anna a guilty glance. "Sorry. Anyway, I think Hoyt's hiding out in your storeroom."

"Is that so?" Irritated, Anna pressed her lips together and cast another despairing glance at the author's table. Mrs. Abercrombie had gone to talk to Coulter. Hopefully, the retired English teacher and Bailey's food delivery would keep Coulter distracted while she went to see what Hoyt was finding so fascinating in her storeroom.

Chapter Seven

"What on earth are you doing up there, Hoyt?"

Balanced on top of the wobbly chair he'd dragged into the middle of the room, Hoyt jumped, banging his head on the light fixture he'd pried loose from the ceiling.

"Don't sneak up on me like that." He steadied himself, feeling the rickety chair tremble beneath him. "This thing's been threatening to break ever since I climbed up on it. If I move around too much, I'm probably going down in a pile of splinters."

"You know what? That might just serve you right." Anna walked into the storage room, her hands fisted on her hips.

She looked a little annoyed.

Hoyt had a sudden flashback to the time he'd been removing a brass chandelier from a building scheduled for demolition. A dusty honeybee had zoomed out of the hole he was making in the plastered ceiling.

It had looked annoyed, too. Hoyt had impatiently swatted it out of the way with his free hand before giving a mighty tug on the stubborn fixture.

Serious mistake. The bee had been immediately joined by about three hundred of his closest friends, swarming out of their secret mammoth hive in the ceiling. Hoyt had ended up with fifteen stings and a sprained ankle from bailing off a twelve-foot ladder.

With that memory in mind, he stepped carefully off the chair. "Is something wrong?"

"Yes, something's wrong! You're not supposed to be in here breaking my poor chairs to smithereens. You're supposed to be out there mingling with the author."

Mingling. Hoyt snorted; then he caught another look at Anna's expression and tried to disguise the noise as a cough. "I thought I'd come in here for a minute and take a closer look at this light. I noticed it flickering when I was finishing up with the window the other day. It's a good thing I checked it out. The wiring up in this ceiling is frayed. You can't be too careful with things like that, especially in an old building like this one. This dry wood would blaze up like a book of matches if it ever caught a spark."

Anna squinted up at the light. Then she glanced over her shoulder at the half-open door. "I appreciate the concern, but this really isn't the time to be taking my storage room apart. I have an important event going on, remember?"

"That's fine. You can go on back." He couldn't resist lifting one eyebrow at her. "*Mingle.* I want to take a closer look at the outlets in here and your electrical panel. I can't do much tonight, but I'd like to get a better idea of what we're dealing with before I talk to the electrician."

Her face fell. "But after the refreshments, we start

the roundtable discussion where people ask questions about the book. You don't want to miss that."

Actually, he kinda did. He didn't say anything, but his expression must have given him away. Anna groaned and plopped herself down on a torn beanbag chair. Its white pellet filling gooshed out on the floor.

"I know! I spent all the money you loaned me on this, and Coulter's *awful*."

She looked so bummed. It made him feel like a jerk for skipping out on the boring lecture. He stood awkwardly over her, shifting a rusty screw he'd taken out of the light fixture from hand to hand. He searched his brain for the right thing to say.

"Well, at least you've got a pretty good crowd in there. That's something."

"I'm not sure why they came. Nobody seems the least bit interested in meeting Coulter or buying his book." Her gaze suddenly zeroed in on his face, and her eyebrows lowered. "What did *you* think of Coulter's book?"

Now that was a loaded question if he'd ever heard one. He got very interested in examining the screw. "I'm probably not the best guy to talk to. I'm not too clear on all that inner conflict stuff he was talking about."

"Did you even read the book, Hoyt?"

He could tell by her tone that she already knew the answer to her question. Hoyt sighed and slipped the screw into his pocket. The jig was up, and he might as well come clean.

"No, I didn't. I meant to. And I tried." He watched as Anna's expression darkened. She opened her mouth, but he hurried on before she could speak. "But come on, Anna, that book—" He stopped, trying to think of some way to describe it that wasn't rude. He came up with nothing. "One thing's for sure. The guy who wrote it doesn't know anything about scaffolding. I thought the whole thing was stupid," he finished honestly.

"That *stupid* book has been on the bestseller lists for a month and a half, Hoyt. And it's received rave reviews from all the most significant literary critics."

"Maybe so." Hoyt shrugged. "One thing you learn in the construction business is that people like strange things. One time a couple asked me to install a claw-foot tub in their dining room. Plumbing and all. They were going to use it to ice down drinks. Painted it bright red, too. People like some weird stuff."

His attempt at distraction didn't work. "Since you didn't even read the book, how do you know if it was weird?"

Their gazes met, and she quirked one narrow, dark eyebrow at him. He blew out a breath. "I read some of it."

"Some of it." Anna shook her head. "I feel like I'm back in high school, wrangling with you over an English assignment."

So did he, and he didn't much care for the memories this particular argument was bringing up. But high school was a long time ago, and things were different now.

He was different now, whether Anna could see that or not.

He met Anna's accusing gaze head-on. "Okay, then. Tell me this. What'd *you* think of it?"

"At least I read it, so I'm entitled to have an opinion about it."

Hoyt studied Anna, who was having an unusual

amount of trouble meeting his eyes. He couldn't help it. He chuckled.

Even a blind squirrel found himself a nut every once in a while.

"You didn't like it, either."

Anna opened her mouth to say something. Then she shut it again and glowered at him.

"Gotcha," he teased.

Anna looked like she was about to explode. "All *right*," she spluttered. "I *didn't* like the book, and the man's an even bigger pompous pain in the neck than he was back in college. And to top things off, now you're telling me this place is one spark away from burning to the ground unless I shell out for a bunch of expensive repairs I can't possibly afford? Tonight's a complete disaster."

"Oh, *my*," Trisha Saunders drawled from the doorway. Hoyt and Anna had been so focused on each other that neither of them had noticed the door being eased fully open. James Coulter stood beside Trisha, glaring at them. He had his plastic-wrapped plate of food in one hand and outrage written all over his face. The look on Trisha's face tended more toward satisfaction. She lifted an eyebrow. "Looks like it's true, what they say, Mr. Coulter. Eavesdroppers really don't hear well of themselves."

"James." Anna had gone white. "I'm so sorry. I had no idea… I didn't mean…"

"Oh, I understood precisely what you meant." The man was swelling up like a toad. "I expected better from you, Anna, I really did. At the very least I expected a certain degree of gratitude after I came all the way to this backwater town just to do an old friend a favor."

"And I appreciate that," Anna started, but Hoyt cut in.

"She paid you to come and bought you that fifty-dollar plate of overpriced snacks you're holding to boot. If anything, she did *you* the favor."

"For your information, I gave her a ten percent discount on my speaking fee, and these aren't even the crackers I asked for!" The author dropped the plate on the ground with an angry flourish. "As far as I'm concerned, this evening is over."

A smile played around Trisha's lips as she stepped aside so the man could storm past her back into the bookstore.

"James! Please wait!" Anna started after him.

Hoyt caught her by the arm before she made it across the threshold. "Let him go, Anna."

"I can't! People expect him to sit and talk with them. Besides, I already paid him."

"I think you're going to have to write that money off. You saw the mood he's in now. If he talks to any of your customers now, trust me, it won't end well. They may want to *throw* his books at him, but they sure won't be buying any of them."

"This isn't funny, Hoyt!"

It was a *little* funny, but he wasn't about to point that out. Anna was chewing on her bottom lip and staring at the door. "Maybe if I just talk to him…"

"Not a good idea." Coulter didn't strike Hoyt as a gentleman. If Anna followed that guy outside, Hoyt suspected he was going to end his own night by punching a bestselling author right in the mouth.

Nobody needed that to happen.

"One spark from burning to the ground? Is that what

you said?" Trisha peered up at the dangling light fixture. "How terrifying!"

Just what he needed right now: Trisha sticking her new-and-improved nose into all this. "Don't go off the deep end, Trish. Anna's wiring will have to be brought up to code, that's all."

"It's not even up to code?" Trish's eyebrows lowered, and she turned to Anna. "You'd better get this firetrap fixed fast. Although if you want to sell the store, I *might* still be interested. Naturally I'd have to amend my offer to account for the cost of all the additional work that's going to have to be done."

"Naturally." There was a strange tone in Anna's voice that made Hoyt shift his attention back in her direction. From the look on her face, Anna was either about to start crying or throwing things. He wasn't sure which. Either way, Trish didn't need to be standing around gawking when it happened.

"Excuse us, Trish. Anna and I need to talk about getting this work scheduled." Hoyt didn't wait to see if Trish planned to cooperate. He herded her out of the storeroom and shut the door in the woman's annoyed face.

"Don't worry about all this, Anna. I work with the best electrical contractor in this area. Mitch Connor and I will get this knocked out in no time." Mitch would pitch in; he always did. There wasn't a whole lot of leeway in their schedules right now, so they'd be looking at a few weeks of evening and weekend work. That didn't matter. He'd manage somehow. "We'll be working at night, and everything will go a lot faster if we can cut the power off. Is there someplace you could stay for a few weeks?" The thought of her sleeping upstairs gave him chills now that he'd gotten a closer look at the tangled mess up in this ceiling.

"I can't."

"It's really not going to cost that much. I'll get the material for you wholesale."

"It doesn't matter." Anna cut him off. "Whatever it costs would be too much. There's no *money*, Hoyt. I spent the whole check you gave me on the author I just insulted—him and those expensive organic snacks he threw all over the floor."

"Anna..."

"I'll have to sell. And now, thanks to you rummaging around in here, where you weren't even supposed to *be*, by the way, Trish is going to lower her offer even more." Anna stopped and pressed her lips together tightly for a second before continuing in a calmer voice. "I guess I should be thankful that you found this problem, but I kind of wish you hadn't. I really don't need anything else to deal with right now. I can't talk about this anymore. I have to go tell people the roundtable isn't happening."

She left the room. A minute later he heard her explaining calmly that Coulter had been forced to leave unexpectedly.

Personally, he doubted anybody out there would be too upset over that news.

Except for Anna.

There'd been something way worse than anger in her eyes just then. He'd seen a broken defeat that he recognized all too well. He knew what that felt like... that desperate sense of being boxed in with nowhere to turn. He'd kind of specialized in that for a while after Marylee died.

The thought of Anna feeling that way… Well, it bothered him. In fact, it more than bothered him. It hit him somewhere deep in his gut, in that place reserved only for a few special people, the people in his world that he'd do pretty much anything for.

He made it a personal point to keep that list short. But when Anna had handed his hurting little girl that shabby stuffed dog, she had crossed deeply into that territory.

He hadn't realized how deeply until this very moment.

He drew in a slow breath and considered the dangling light fixture. He had a lot of things to think about.

Not the bookstore repairs. He already knew what he was going to do about those. That crazy wiring had to be fixed and soon. That was a no-brainer.

But figuring out what he was going to do about his feelings for Anna Delaney? That was likely to take a while.

"Now, then." Mabel Abercrombie finished arranging a display of mysteries on a small table and stepped back to squint at her work. "That just about does it. You're all ready to open up tomorrow morning." The trim African American woman dusted her hands briskly and glanced at her watch. "Barely ten o'clock, too. We've been very efficient."

"I appreciate your help." Anna tucked the last chair back into place under a scarred library table.

"Oh, I've quite enjoyed it, my dear. If you ask me, retirement's overrated. I do enjoy a good project. The next time you plan an event like this, let me know. I'll be delighted to come and help you."

"I'm afraid there's not going to be a next time." Anna picked up a bottle of James Coulter's special brand of sparkling water and chucked it into the trash. Hard. "This was a disaster." She picked up a damp cloth and began wiping off the table.

"I think perhaps you need to review the definition of *disaster*, Anna. In any case, you mustn't be discouraged. The man was a bore, and his book certainly didn't live up to its reviews, but that's hardly your fault. On the other hand, you got twenty Pine Valley residents interested in a literary event, including Hoyt Bradley." The older woman chuckled. "And did I hear that he actually *sponsored* this? As his former English teacher, I'd consider that a resounding success."

Anna picked up a garbage bag stuffed with paper plates and half-eaten treats. She twisted the top closed with more force than was actually necessary. "I wouldn't get too excited about Hoyt, Mrs. Abercrombie. For him, this is more about helping Jess than it is about promoting literature. He didn't even finish reading the book."

"He started it?" Her former teacher laughed again. "That's a great deal more than I would have expected. Unfortunately, Hoyt's never had much time to devote to reading. He's always been focused on other things."

"Like sports, you mean." Anna plopped the cinched garbage bag by the door. She'd take it out to the dumpster tomorrow morning.

It took her a second to realize that Mrs. Abercrombie hadn't answered. She looked up to see the other woman studying her. Her former teacher wore an expression that made Anna feel as if she'd just turned in a paper with a run-on sentence.

"No," Mrs. Abercrombie corrected quietly. "I mean like survival."

As Anna met her teacher's unflinching brown eyes, Mrs. Abercrombie made a soft tsking sound with her tongue. "My dear girl, you were the finest literature student I ever had the pleasure to teach, but I'm afraid you've always read books far better than you read people."

Anna frowned. "What do you mean?"

"Come sit down with me for a second." When they were settled at the table, Mrs. Abercrombie tilted back her head, looking at Anna through the bottom of her glasses. "You did know, of course, that Hoyt's father was an alcoholic?"

"Everybody in town knew that."

"Yes. What everybody didn't know was that from the time Hoyt was about twelve years old, he was functioning as the responsible adult in his family. His mother, God rest her soul, was such a *scatterbrained* woman." Mrs. Abercrombie pursed her lips disapprovingly. "Quite incapable. I tried to help Alicia Bradley myself on several separate occasions, but she never could muster up the gumption to leave her husband. No," the older woman continued, "Hoyt got every scrap of the backbone in that family. By the time he was in high school, he was managing the majority of his father's construction business, too. Of course his schoolwork suffered, but Hoyt had very little choice, I'm afraid."

"That's terrible."

"Yes, it was. And though I never could prove it, I always suspected there were other issues going on in that home, as well. Far worse ones." The retired teacher fell silent, but something in her expression made a shiver run across Anna's shoulders.

"I didn't know."

"Nobody knew the whole of it because Hoyt ensured they were kept in the dark. He wanted nobody's pity and nobody's interference. A lot of young men would have been destroyed by such problems, but not Hoyt. In fact, in all the time I've known him, I've only seen Hoyt Bradley brought to his knees once."

Anna nodded slowly. "When Marylee died."

"Yes. He took that loss very hard. For a time I worried that… Well, no matter. Those fears came to nothing, thankfully. Hoyt bobbed back up to the surface, just like he always has. He set his own grief aside to help that dear little girl of his. As I've said, I've found retirement overrated, so I volunteer at the pre-K program. I've had plenty of opportunities to watch Hoyt advocating for Jess. He never seemed to care all that much about his own schooling, but Jess's education is certainly a top priority for him. No father could have done more, I assure you. Personally I've found it all quite heroic."

"Heroic? *Hoyt?*"

"Precisely." A little smile flickered across Mrs. Abercrombie's face. "Perhaps that's another definition you need to review, my dear. I believe a person could learn a great deal from a man like Hoyt Bradley. If she paid close attention, that is. Now, then. I'd best be getting myself along home." Mrs. Abercrombie stood. She leaned down and laid her hand gently over Anna's. "We teachers plant seeds, you know. Hundreds of them. Some take longer to germinate than others, that's all.

But it's never too late to learn something new." She smiled. "Good night, Anna."

After Mrs. Abercrombie had gone, Anna remained at the table, tracing the wood grain with one finger, mulling over what her former teacher had said.

Heroic. *Hoyt Bradley.*

Go figure.

"Wow." Hoyt whistled through his teeth as he scanned the sketches Abel Whitlock had unrolled on the makeshift desk in the work trailer. "That mantelpiece is absolutely amazing. My customer's going to be over the moon. No wonder your business has taken off."

Abel's mouth tilted up in a crooked smile. "I'm obliged to you for the referral. I'm looking to stay busy now that I've got some new mouths to feed."

"How are Emily and those new twins of yours?"

"Doing just fine." The other man's expression softened. "All fat and sassy, just like they should be."

Hoyt laughed, and Abel's lean cheeks colored red.

"The *babies* are fat, I mean. Not Emily." A look of panic crossed Abel's weathered face. "I don't reckon I'll ever quit stumbling over my own tongue."

"Hoyt?" Mitch Connor stuck his head into the trailer. "There's a lady out here asking for you, if you've got a minute."

This was shaping up to be another crazy morning. "I don't have a minute, but I'll see her anyway. Thanks for bringing the sketches by, Abel."

"No problem. And you won't…uh…repeat that little slip I just made to Emily?"

Hoyt grinned. "Not unless you get on my bad side."

As Abel opened the flimsy door to leave, he stepped

politely aside, nodding to the woman who was mounting the shaky wooden steps. "Morning, Miss Anna."

"Good morning, Abel." Anna edged past him and looked around the cluttered trailer. "Hi, Hoyt. So this is where you work?"

"For now." Hoyt rerolled Abel's sketches and secured them with a rubber band. He'd run them out to the customers later, but there was no big rush. He knew he'd get the go-ahead once the wife got a look at Abel's plans. "We can move it to whatever work site we're on, so it's convenient. One of these days, though, I'm going to have a real office." He set the sketches to the side and drew in a deep breath. "I'm glad you stopped by, Anna. I think I owe you an apology."

"No, you don't."

"I told you I'd read that book and attend your thing. I didn't follow through. I'm sorry."

"Please don't worry about it." Anna brushed the apology away with a quick gesture. "I'm the one who was in the wrong. You were right about the book. It wasn't a good choice. I don't blame you for not finishing it."

This was unexpected. "Well, I probably shouldn't have gone elbow-deep in your ceiling while Trisha Saunders was nosing around, either."

"I'd rather have had an opportunity to deal with the problem before Trisha found out about it, yes. But if it's a serious concern, it's a good thing to know about. Not that I can afford to do anything about it. Not right now, anyway."

Alarm stabbed at him. "Anna, look. I understand you're in a tight spot financially, but this really isn't anything to play around with. That wiring—"

"Has been in the building since it was built and

hasn't caused a problem yet," Anna finished his sentence for him. "I'm not saying it won't have to be dealt with at some point. I'll just have to pray it doesn't catch fire until I can afford to have it repaired or I sell the building, whichever comes first."

Hoyt believed in the power of prayer, but he also believed in using common sense. Still, he couldn't force Anna to fix the wiring, no matter how much he wanted to.

But the city inspector could. Knowing Trish like he did, he imagined the whole mess would be taken out of Anna's hands before long anyway.

He let a beat of silence fall between them and then sighed. "So what can I do for you, Anna?"

"Actually I came by to ask you for a favor."

"Anything." He meant it. "Do you need money? Because I'll be glad to—"

"No! I'm not about to let you throw more of your money away. I don't even know how I'm going to pay you back for that other loan now."

"You don't have to. Consider it a gift."

"Hoyt."

"Call it a lease payment on Chester, then. That dog's worth a million dollars as far as I'm concerned. I still feel bad about you giving something that special to Jess. And I want you to know, I'm going to return it to you, just as soon as I can."

"Don't bother." Anna made an exasperated noise. "As far as I'm concerned, Jess is welcome to him. And I'm certainly not going to let you pay me rent on the stupid thing."

Hoyt raised his eyebrows. *Stupid thing.* Chester? Something wasn't adding up here, and given the elaborate pay-Anna-back plan he'd already set in motion, he'd better figure out what was going on. "But something like that's irreplaceable. I mean, a toy your mom gave you right before she died…that's something you'd want to hang on to."

"She didn't give him to me."

"What? I thought you said—"

"I said that's what my father told me. It wasn't true. He lied."

"I don't understand."

"Neither did I. Until I found my dad's journal a few months ago. Apparently he lied about a lot of things where my mother was concerned. That trip she was on when she died? It was one way. She was moving to France to be with some man she met at a conference. She was leaving my father. She was leaving both of us."

"What?"

"He didn't want me to be…hurt, so he made up this big story. He told me she was going to visit long-lost relatives, and he bought me a stuffed dog and said it was from her." Anna shrugged shortly. "But none of it was real, and I can promise you I don't care a thing about that dog now. Jess is welcome to him. Anyway, Chester isn't what I came to talk to you about. I wondered if you'd be willing to give me some professional networking lessons."

"Professional networking?" He was still trying to wrap his brain around what she'd just told him, but he did his best to switch directions. "You mean like with computers?"

"No, that's not what I meant. I'm thinking more locally than that."

"Locally." He repeated the word, puzzled.

"Yes, I think you were right in what you told me before. Improving my perspective on the local community could have a positive impact on my business."

Light dawned. As usual, Anna was throwing five-dollar words at a two-dollar problem. "You want me to help you make some *friends* with other business owners around here? Is that what you're saying?"

Color flushed into her face, just the pink of the wild roses that were climbing all over his pasture fence this time of year. Whenever Anna Delaney blushed she was the prettiest woman in Pine Valley, no two ways about it.

"Yes, but you can probably cross Trisha Saunders off the short list since I'm doing this to avoid selling her the building. I have to warn you, though. Socializing has never been my strongest skill. You'll have your work cut out for you, trying to teach me." The smile she offered him was stiff, and she'd twisted her hands together so tightly that her knuckles were white.

The expression on her face reminded him of an afternoon last fall when Jess had tried riding her two-wheeler bike for the first time. She'd fallen off about six pedals in and skinned her elbow. After he'd finished bandaging her up, Jess stomped over to the garage and dragged her tricycle out.

It had taken Hoyt two solid months to get his daughter back on that two-wheeler.

Anna didn't need another setback right now. She needed a sure thing. An idea occurred to him.

"Tomorrow night I'm going for pizza with a group of business owners in the area, guys we went to high school with. We get together every few months or so and brainstorm ways to cross-promote our businesses. You should come."

"Are you sure?"

"Yeah." He was sure. Wasn't he? "Mitch and I will be by your place around six."

"Mitch Connor? Isn't he the electrician you work with?"

Hoyt grinned. Nothing got by Anna Delaney.

"Yeah. And he's going to look over your place and come up with an estimate while we're out. Plus, he's going to install you a state-of-the-art smoke alarm. Nope." She'd opened her mouth to protest. "That's the deal. An estimate's free, and it's always better to know what you're up against. And the smoke alarm's a non-negotiable gift from me. Trisha might be trying to cheat you, but she does have one halfway decent point on her side. There are other buildings attached to yours, so you're not the only person who could be injured if that wiring goes up. There needs to be an alert that goes out to the fire department if anything happens before the repairs can be made. Mitch can set the alarm to send an alert to your cell phone. Mine, too, unless you have a problem with that. It's always good to have more than one phone number programmed in, just in case."

She hesitated and then nodded. "Okay. I guess you have a point. As long as Mr. Connor's only giving an estimate, at least for now. And if you're sure your friends won't mind me tagging along with you."

"Are you kidding? Like I said, we all went to high school together. They'll be glad to see you again."

Anna flashed a skeptical smile at him, her cheeks still that rosy pink. "If you say so."

As her eyes met his, something buried deep in his

chest rolled over and came to life for the first time in years. Suddenly there seemed to be too much space between them—and too little—all at the same time.

The feeling was both strange and familiar. He'd felt it before, sure, but not for years, and only ever with one woman.

He was starting to think these weird feelings he was having for Anna Delaney ran even deeper than he'd thought.

Maybe a lot deeper.

And he had absolutely no idea what to do with that.

Chapter Eight

Tino's Pizzeria had been around forever. Sporting red-and-white-checkered tablecloths and fat white candles flickering in the center of little tables, Tino's was the closest thing to fine dining Pine Valley had to offer. As long as she could remember, it had been the high school hot spot for dating and hanging out.

Anna had only been there a handful of times, usually to pick up takeout for her and her father. She remembered standing uncomfortably in front of the high, polished counter, breathing in the heavy scent of Tino's signature sauce, acutely aware of the laughter and loud talking coming from the tables of her classmates in the back.

They hadn't been laughing at her. She knew that. They probably hadn't even noticed she was in the room. But she'd been glad when her father had decided to drop some weight and had cut pizza and pasta out of his diet.

She'd never felt very much at home at Tino's.

"Anna? Are you all right?" Startled, she glanced over to find Hoyt watching her from the driver's seat. "Sorry. You had a funny look on your face, and you haven't unfastened your seat belt." He lowered his voice. "Don't get freaked out, okay? This is just dinner with old friends. No big deal." He raised his voice. "What about you, Jess? You ready for some pizza?"

"Pizza!" Jess sang out from the back seat of the truck. She kicked her pink tennis shoes against the base of her booster seat. "Pizza with Miss Bailey!"

"That's right, kiddo. Bailey's running a little late, so you'll have to hang out with Daddy and Anna for a few minutes, okay?"

"Okay!"

"So? You good to go?" Hoyt looked back at Anna. His hazel eyes twinkled as he nodded toward the seat belt. "Or should I ask Tino to bring your pizza out here?"

"Ha ha." Anna pressed the silver button, and the canvas strap slid free.

"Let's go."

Hoyt was out of the truck in a flash. Anna reached for her own door handle and then hesitated. She never knew what to do these days. Did she open her own door or wait for the man to do it? It was awkward.

But this wasn't a date. And Hoyt had to get Jess out of her car seat. Of course she should open her own door.

She pushed, but Hoyt caught the handle before she'd opened it halfway. He pulled the door the rest of the way open, even offering her a steadying hand as she climbed down from his big truck onto the sidewalk. "What? Now you're in a hurry all of a sudden?"

He was teasing, but Anna flushed. She should've waited. Maybe Hoyt's upbringing had been on the rough side, but he'd been born and raised in Pine Valley, where old-fashioned manners were the norm. Of course he'd expect to open doors for any woman he was driving somewhere. She should have known that.

She never got this stuff right.

While Hoyt unfastened his daughter's safety straps, Anna focused on the multipaned wooden door leading into the pizzeria. There was a sidewalk sign close by, listing the daily specials and displaying a colored chalk pizza with a big slice missing. From the look of it, it was the same old sign Tino had been using for decades. Even way out here she could hear laughter coming from inside, and her heart beat harder.

She was going to blow this. She just knew it.

"Miss Anna?" Jess wiggled insistent fingers in her direction. The little girl was already holding Hoyt's hand, but she wanted Anna's, as well. "Let's go get some pizza!"

She took Jess's hand, feeling the little girl's slightly sticky fingers twine trustingly around her own. Hoyt's eyes met hers, and he grinned.

That grin had the butterflies in Anna's stomach multiplying like rabbits. She knew why Hoyt was smiling. Jess was talking. That warm light in his eyes was all about his daughter. It had nothing to do with Anna.

But for a second, standing there, feeling tiny fingers in hers and seeing Hoyt's face soften in that smile, it sure felt more...personal.

It felt like family.

Don't go there, she warned herself. The last thing she needed right now was any more crazy feelings added to what she was already dealing with.

Tonight is all about making some useful business connections. Focus on that.

She gave Jess's hand a quick squeeze and forced herself to smile at Hoyt. "Any last-minute tips, Coach?"

"This isn't a chemistry final, Delaney. It's just pizza with some old friends. Nobody needs tips for that."

Maybe nobody else did. "Okay, then. I'm ready."

Hoyt didn't move. He was looking at her thoughtfully, his head tilted slightly to one side. Anna frowned. "What?"

"You could take your hair down, maybe."

"My hair?" Anna reached up with her free hand and touched the side of her head carefully. What was wrong with her hair? She'd spent the better part of an hour trying to straighten the curly mess, but that flat iron she'd bought hadn't been up to the task. She'd finally given up and pulled it up into something vaguely resembling a French twist.

Not her first choice, but she thought she'd done a fair job. Her hair never looked great, but at least with it up she didn't look like some kind of frizzy-headed freak.

"You look more comfortable when it's not all scraped back from your face like that. Here." Before she could react, he released Jess's hand, reached around behind Anna's head and gently pulled out the clips she'd wedged in.

Anna gasped as her mass of hair tumbled around her shoulders. The destruction of her carefully crafted hairstyle wasn't the only reason. There was something a little too…cozy about the gesture.

"There!" Hoyt sounded satisfied. "That's much better, don't you think, Jess?"

"Yes! Now she looks bee-*you*-tiful!" The little girl beamed up at Anna and tugged hard on her hand. "Can we *please* get pizza now?"

"Sure thing," Hoyt said cheerfully. "Here, Anna, could you chuck these gizmos in your purse? Let's go on in."

Anna stopped frantically finger-combing her hair one-handed long enough to accept her hair clips. She could only imagine what she looked like now.

Hoyt was already holding the door open. She'd just have to—what was that expression Hoyt was so fond of? *Roll with it.* She dropped the clips in her purse and went through the door.

Those psychologists weren't kidding when they said that scents were the most powerful memory boosters in the world. One sniff and Anna was right back in high school. She even found herself running her tongue across her front teeth to see if her spiky braces were truly gone.

Her heart kept up its nervous hammering as the three of them threaded their way toward the back of the small restaurant. Part of that was Hoyt's fault, though. He'd left her holding Jess's hand and had placed his on the small of Anna's back, steering her through the crowded tangle of tables and chairs with a gentle pressure. She was way too aware of that solid warmth on the middle of her spine.

It was distracting.

She edged to the side in an attempt to politely dislodge his hand and ended up bumping an empty chair over onto the red-tiled floor. It fell directly into the path of a waitress, who stepped back, her laden tray wobbling dangerously.

"Look out, honey!"

"I'm so sorry," Anna apologized. The waitress tossed her an irritated glance as she stepped around the chair.

Apparently Tino's still wasn't her place.

Hoyt leaned closer, his breath puffing warmly against her ear. "Take it easy there, champ. Here we are."

It took her only a second or two to recognize the three men sitting at the table. For one thing, they hadn't changed much since high school, and for another, as star athletes, they'd all been in the top tier of the social pecking order back then.

Everybody had known their names.

The one on the end there, with his long legs stuck out in the aisle, was Jimmy "Stork" Martin. He'd been as important to the basketball team as Hoyt had been to the football team. The baseball team was represented by ex-pitcher Bobby Finch, who had his chair tilted back on two legs and was wearing an Atlanta Braves cap low on his head. Carl Langston, the wrestling champion, had changed the most. He'd gotten a lot heavier and was eyeing the basket of breadsticks with the passion of a guy whose wife had him on a diet.

Well, the thing she'd dreamed about every lunch hour in tenth grade had finally happened. Hoyt Bradley had invited her to sit with the popular kids.

"You guys remember Anna Delaney." Hoyt wasn't asking a question, she realized. He was telling them they remembered her. She smiled at the men, who smiled politely back.

No, of course, they didn't remember her, not really. A girl like her would never have been on their radar. But with Hoyt looming over them, they weren't about to admit it.

"I'm going to go grab us some sweet tea," Hoyt said. He glanced at Carl, who had caved and was double dipping a bitten breadstick into the marinara sauce. "And another basket of breadsticks. Carl, you're disgusting, man. Come on, Jess. Bailey says you can pick out the pizza for the to-go order."

Jess nodded. She didn't speak, but she released Anna's hand and fluttered her fingers at her father, who swung the tiny girl up into his arms.

"We'll be right back."

"Okay," Anna smiled tensely. "Sure." *Sure. Leave me alone with these guys right off the bat. That's a great idea.*

She wasn't the only one feeling uncomfortable. The men looked at each other uneasily. Jimmy stood up and pulled out a chair.

"I'm forgetting my manners. Have a seat, Anna. You'll have to excuse us. We're not used to having ladies at these little meetings."

"Not true," Carl mumbled around a mouthful of bread. "Bailey comes sometimes."

"Bailey's different." Bobby spoke up from his corner. "And you better be glad she's not here tonight, Carl, because she'd climb your frame about those breadsticks." The ex-pitcher turned to Anna. "Bradley says you want to brainstorm some ideas for cross-promoting your bookstore."

"Yes. I—" Anna began, but Carl interrupted.

"But don't people just buy their books online now? I mean, you can have books shipped right to your house these days, can't you?"

"How would you know?" Jimmy asked with a snort. "When was the last time you bought a book?"

"I hear stuff, don't I?" Carl inquired airily. "Besides, my wife reads. But she has one of those electronic thingies, you know. Like a tablet, but with books on it. She likes those better. She doesn't want a lot of books cluttering up the house."

Books were clutter? Anna struggled to keep her smile in place. "E-readers and online shopping are huge nowadays, that's true. But if you ask me, there's something special about brick-and-mortar bookstores and the feel of an actual book in your hand." There. At least she'd squeezed in part of the sales pitch she'd been rehearsing.

"I guess. But it still sounds like a pretty risky business to be in these days. Kind of like trying to sell people cassette tapes or something. What?" Carl turned to Jimmy. "What're you elbowing me for, Stork?"

"That bookstore belonged to her *dad*, Carl," Jimmy muttered between his teeth. "Remember what Hoyt said? She's Principal Delaney's daughter. It's a family business."

"Sorry," Carl mumbled. "I didn't mean anything by that."

"That's fine. It was a valid question."

"I was really sorry to hear about your father's death," Jimmy said. "That must have been hard."

"Thank you. It was."

"Mr. Delaney was a good egg," Jimmy continued. "I can't believe he's gone. He was the high school's principal forever."

"I'll tell you one thing. I still think about him every time I see a man wearing a bow tie." Bobby chuckled. "You never saw Principal Delaney without one. Or those nerdy saddle oxfords.We used to rag him about those shoes all the time, remember?" The ex-pitcher shook his head. "Man, we sure gave that poor guy fits."

"He brought most of that on himself," Carl argued

around a mouthful of bread. "The man had, like, zero sense of humor. He didn't have a whole lot of school spirit, either. Remember that time he gave us detention for skipping world history during homecoming week?" The three men laughed. Carl went on, "And so we broke into his office and sawed the legs off his desk?"

"You guys did that?" Anna's mouth dropped open. She meant it as an accusation, but the men seemed to think she was paying them a compliment.

"That was nothing compared to some of the other stunts we pulled," Bobby interrupted. "What about that time he made Coach suspend us for ungentlemanly behavior?"

"Oh, wow. After we egged that smart-mouthed Eagle mascot at the big Fairmont baseball game?"

"That mascot was the Fairmont coach's twelve-year-old son, dressed up," Anna interjected. She couldn't believe the direction this conversation had taken. This definitely wasn't what she'd signed up for.

"We didn't know that until afterward," Stork put in sheepishly. "The usual guy chickened out at the last minute."

"You hit that poor boy with six dozen eggs."

"Eight dozen, and he had it coming, believe me," Carl said. "You should have heard the stuff he was saying to the players. Delaney totally overreacted. We were suspended for a whole week, and he made us stay after school for a month after that, helping the janitors clean up."

"That boy was really upset. And Fairmont had to throw the Eagle costume away. My dad had to send them the money to buy a new one."

"We got ours, though. Remember, guys?" Carl

snorted. "We called Gina's Florist pretending to be Delaney and ordered a dozen roses and a love note for the meanest lunchroom lady in the cafeteria. We had them delivered in the middle of senior lunch." The two other men shot sidelong glances at each other. They didn't laugh out loud this time, but Anna could see the smiles playing around their mouths.

"Now, that one really wasn't funny. She reported it to the superintendent, and there was an inquiry. My father had to prove that he hadn't acted inappropriately. He could have lost his job."

"We never thought it would go that far," Jimmy put in quickly. "We figured the lady would know it was just a joke."

"Well, she didn't." Anna could remember how unhappy her father had been about that one. Unsurprisingly, he'd been more worried about the outraged lunchroom worker than about himself. What had her name been? Karen something. Her dad had fretted that she might quit over it, and she'd needed the income. "That *joke* caused a lot of trouble. It was almost as bad as when…wait a minute." Another unpleasant memory struck her, and she looked suspiciously at the trio. "Which one of you signed him up for that online dating site?"

All three men immediately dissolved into helpless snickers.

"It's nothing to laugh about! You gave out our home address!"

"None of us did that, Anna," Stork spoke quickly, but there was something in his face that made her narrow her eyes.

"No? Then who was it?"

"That one was all Bradley's idea." Carl yelped as Jimmy elbowed him again. "Oh, come on! What's she going to do about it now? Give him detention? Besides, the man deserves credit. That one was epic. Remember what he wrote in the profile? *Appearance and age not important.*" Carl and Bobby chuckled, and now even Jimmy was fighting back a smile.

"One of those women came to our house. Did you know that? Repeatedly. She was emotionally unstable. Dad couldn't reason with her. He finally had to call the sheriff to come pick her up." Anna stood. She'd had enough of this. "And do you know, he actually felt *bad* about doing that? He did. Because my father was a good man who devoted his entire life to helping people who obviously didn't have enough sense to appreciate him." The men abruptly stopped laughing.

"Sorry, Anna," Jimmy said quickly. "We didn't mean to make you mad."

"What are you sorry for?" Hoyt was standing behind her chair, two large red plastic glasses of tea in his hands. He glanced from the red-faced men to Anna and back again. "What's going on?"

Jess wasn't with him, and Anna saw Bailey Quinn standing with the little girl at the cash register, accepting a big pizza box from the clerk. "You know what? It turns out I'm not in the mood for pizza after all. I'll catch a ride home with Bailey."

Hoyt frowned and set down the sweating glasses of tea. "Hang on just a minute, Anna. What were you guys talking about just now?"

"You can stay here, Hoyt, and let the guys tell you all about it. The four of you can have one last laugh at my dad's expense." Before Hoyt could react, Anna slipped past him and headed for the door Bailey and Jess had just exited.

As she hurried across the parking lot to catch up with them, Anna felt more stupid than she had in years. She should have known better. She should never have agreed to come to Tino's in the first place. Nothing had changed around here.

Nothing at all.

"Look, Hoyt. We're sorry, all right? We were just telling some stories." Bobby had his eyes fixed on Hoyt's face. "We didn't mean anything by it."

Hoyt made a frustrated noise. "You guys were talking about stupid pranks we pulled on the woman's dead father. In what universe is that funny? None of us should be laughing about the dumb things we did back then anyway. I've grown up enough to be ashamed of them. I thought you guys had, too."

"You're right." Jimmy spoke up immediately. "I'd hate to think one of my kids would act like we did in high school."

"Same here," Hoyt agreed. "And Anna's never been the kind who'd laugh at stuff like that, anyway. You remember what she was like back in high school. She's always been serious."

"We didn't know her all that well, Hoyt. I mean, I knew she tutored you in English or whatever and you stood up for her during that cheating thing, but that's about all I remember." Bobby's face, like Jimmy's, was creased with concern. "I'm really sorry."

"I don't remember her at all." Carl swirled another bitten breadstick in the marinara sauce. "I can tell you one thing, though. She can't have been that cute back in high school, or she'd have gotten my attention for sure."

Hoyt's gaze cut sharply in Carl's direction. Bobby took one look at Hoyt's expression, took off his Braves cap and whapped the ex-wrestler on the head with it.

"Shut up, Langston, before you get yourself punched in the mouth. Look, we're really sorry, Bradley. We seriously messed up. What else can we say?"

Hoyt's attention had been drawn to the sliver of parking lot he could see through Tino's checkered curtains. Anna was getting into Bailey's truck. Bailey would see Anna safely home, so that much was good.

But then Hoyt was going to have to go see her and do some serious groveling on behalf of these bozos. And himself, thanks to their big mouths.

Not good.

He glared at his friends. Stork and Bobby looked genuinely concerned, but Carl was still zeroed in on the breadsticks. It didn't matter. He was equally irritated with all of them.

"Anna Delaney kept me on the football team when football was the only good thing I had in my life."

His tone got even Carl's attention. He paused mid-chew.

Hoyt kept going. "She did it in spite of me, too. I wasn't much help. I was too wrapped up in what was going on at home to focus much on school." The men shot long, silent looks at each other. They knew exactly what had been going on at Hoyt's house back then. "Looking back now, I see what a difference being on that team made. If Anna hadn't pulled it off…if I'd been cut from the team at that point in my life… I don't know what I would have done."

"Look, like I said, we're all really sorry," Bobby said earnestly. "Aren't we, guys?"

"Yeah," Stork promptly agreed. Bobby shot an elbow into Carl's ribs, and he coughed.

"Yeah. Sorry, Bradley."

"I'm not the one you owe the apology to. You all should go apologize to Anna, like I'm planning to do. But just saying we're sorry's not going to be enough this time."

"We get that, Hoyt, but what else can we do?" Bobby asked. "Tell us, and it's done. Okay?"

Hoyt craned his neck to look out the window again. Bailey's truck was crunching out of the parking lot. He turned back to the table. "You can buy some books, that's what you can do."

There was a long beat of silence.

"Books?" Stork repeated finally.

"Lots of 'em. You know where Delaney's bookstore is. Just off the town square. You're all—" Hoyt looked hard at each of them in turn "—going to go buy books. Like tomorrow. And I mean, you're going to drop some serious cash. Understood?"

"Yep." Stork nodded. "We're all buying books. First thing tomorrow. You have our word on it. Doesn't he?"

"Sure thing," Bobby agreed. "Books. Lots of them."

"That's not all. You're going to see how else you can help her. Boost her business some. Maybe you can do some joint sales with your car lot, Stork. She has some of those things—those books you can listen to while you're driving. You could throw one of those in with every car purchase." When Stork nodded, Hoyt turned to his next victim. "And Bobby, you're always looking for things to give away as prizes at the radio station. How about some gift certificates for books from Anna's store?"

"I usually get those prizes donated, Hoyt. Folks give them to me free for promotional—" Bobby trailed off. "But sure. I could buy some gift certificates, I guess. In fact, I'll be happy to."

"And Carl, you can—" Hoyt stalled out as he looked at the expectant face in front of him. Carl was the local exterminator. Hoyt tried to think of some way Carl could connect Anna's store with his business, but he came up with a big bunch of nothing. "You can buy books."

"Lots of them," Bobby repeated sternly.

Carl shrugged. "If you say so." As Hoyt turned to head for the door, he heard Carl mutter, "But what am I going to do with a bunch of *books*?"

Hoyt didn't bother to answer. Finding a use for the books was Carl's problem. The only thing that mattered to Hoyt right now was smoothing things over with Anna.

Chapter Nine

"Grab a slice, Anna." Bailey Quinn settled Jess at a table in the back of her gourmet grocery store with a big triangle of Tino's famous thin-crust pepperoni. Yanking off a generous swath of paper towels, she tucked them in the little girl's collar. "There you go, sweet girl. Slop sauce to your heart's content. I'm going to turn on the television here and you can watch that puppy show you like while Miss Anna and I talk. Okay?" Jess nodded happily.

"No, thanks, Bailey. I need to get going. I have some things to do at Pages." Anna had only planned to hitch a ride, not crash Bailey and Jess's pizza party.

"I hear you. There's always plenty to do when you're running a business. That's why we're eating here. After pizza, I have to spend a couple of hours checking inventory. But all that can wait for half an hour." She flipped the cardboard top open and flopped generous slices on two plates. "Come on. Friends don't make friends eat fattening stuff all alone. It's in the handbook."

Anna hesitated. The smell of the pizza was awfully tempting, and her empty stomach grumbled hopefully.

Then there was that whole *friends* comment Bailey had tossed off so casually. Anna's heart reacted to that every bit as hungrily. The bookstore was only a short walk away.

"I guess I have time for some pizza." She started to pull out another chair at the little table, but Bailey stopped her with a shake of her head and a significant glance in Jess's direction.

"Not here. Grab those water bottles and come with me. We'll eat out in the store. We have some things to talk about." A pizza-laden plate in each hand, Bailey led the way out of the crowded storeroom and headed toward the front.

Anna sighed. She should have escaped when she'd had the chance. She picked up the water bottles and followed.

Bailey settled them down on two high stools at the high counter of her store and pushed a plate in Anna's direction, along with a precautionary paper towel.

"Here. Tino always goes a little crazy with his toppings. Now tell me. What happened back at the restaurant? *Aaank*." When Anna started to speak, Bailey made a noise like a buzzer and held up a warning hand. "Don't say *nothing*. You ran out of there like a scalded cat. What did those guys do?"

Nothing was exactly what Anna had been planning to say. She'd never known Bailey Quinn all that well. Anna remembered her as a chubby girl with an overbite and glasses who'd huddled into the background almost as much as Anna had.

Now Bailey possessed a fit, athletic build and a confident gleam in her perfectly corrected smile. At some point over the years, she'd grown comfortable in her own skin, and she'd certainly made a huge success of her gourmet grocery store, Bailey's, which had recently been featured in a Georgia magazine article spotlighting up-and-coming female entrepreneurs.

Considering that Anna hadn't come close to pulling anything like that off herself, she'd felt intimidated around Bailey since returning to Pine Valley. Still, the other woman's sharp dark eyes were kind, and there was something so chummy about sitting down together with greasy slices of pizza. Before she knew it, Anna was telling the whole sorry tale.

Bailey listened, slowly nibbling her way through her slice of pizza. When she finished the last crisp bite of crust, she sighed with satisfaction. "I've *got* to talk Tino into sharing his secret sauce recipe with me. If we could bottle that stuff we'd make a fortune."

She wadded up her paper towel and took a deep breath. "Listen, butting into other people's business is a bad habit, and I wouldn't blame you a bit if you told me off and stormed out of here. But I'm sure the guys didn't mean to upset you. Stork and Bobby are decent folks, and I'm positive they're feeling lower than algae right now." Bailey's perfect smile flashed. "Carl's kind of a goob, but even he's probably feeling pretty bad, too, if Hoyt has anything to do with it." She leaned back against the store's whitewashed shiplap wall. "Trust me. They'll all behave themselves better next time, and if Hoyt wants them to help you out with your store, they will. They listen to him."

"I'm not sure I want them to."

"Sure you do. I'll help, too. You and I will have ourselves a sit-down soon, and we'll figure out ways Bailey's and Pages can boost each other up."

It was nice of Bailey to phrase it that way…*boost each other up*, as if Anna's floundering store and Bailey's flourishing one were on the same playing field. "You don't have to do that."

"Don't be silly. I'd have offered before if I'd had any idea you'd take me up on it. I'm a big believer in supporting local businesses, for obvious reasons. Plus, you and I are friends." Bailey lifted one dark eyebrow. "Or we're going to be. Right?"

Anna's heart warmed. Bailey was well known to be a straight shooter. If she said something, she meant it. "I'd like that."

"Good. And as your friend, I'm asking you to give the guys another chance. They gave your dad a hard time back in high school, sure. We all did. To be fair, he gave us plenty of ammunition. Those ties, the shoes and that awful comb-over. Remember?" Bailey smiled. "But those were the things that made him lovable, too. Deep down we were all crazy about him."

"I hope you're right, but it sure didn't sound that way. My dad gave his whole life to this town, but it seemed like he was nothing but a joke to them. Even Hoyt." Anna set her pizza slice down. She'd lost her appetite.

"Your dad was joked *with*. But he was never looked on as a joke." Bailey spoke with conviction. "Especially not by Hoyt. He thought the world of your father."

"He had a funny way of showing it, then. I had no idea Hoyt was behind that dating site disaster. We dodged some of those poor women for months. And then there was the whole test keys mess. That could have destroyed my dad's career. As it was, I nearly lost the Hayes scholarship over it. And Hoyt *did* lose his scholarship to UGA."

The confidence vanished from Bailey's expression, replaced by a shell-shocked uncertainty. "Hoyt Bradley didn't take those test keys, Anna."

Anna blinked. "Of course he did. He admitted to it."

"No, he never did. He just didn't deny it."

"Same thing." Anna had proclaimed her own innocence from the rooftops, not that many people had believed her. If Hoyt hadn't been guilty, surely he'd have done that, too. Maybe he hadn't come right out and confessed. Apart from trying to clear Anna, he'd just been stoically silent throughout the whole mess. Anna had taken that silence as a tacit admission of guilt.

"It isn't the same thing at all." Bailey hesitated. "I'm not sure this story is mine to tell. But I'll tell you this much. I know for a fact that Hoyt didn't steal those keys." She made a short, disbelieving noise. "I can't believe we're even having this conversation. I mean, surely you don't care about all that *now*?"

You're kind of going for a gold medal in grudge-holding, Delaney. Hoyt's words replayed themselves in Anna's memory.

But she *did* care, and she wanted to know the truth. If Hoyt hadn't stolen those answer sheets, it…changed things.

"And you're *sure* that Hoyt didn't take them?"

"Yes." Bailey's answer was immediate and firm. "I'm positive, Anna."

"Then who did?"

"Somebody I was…close to." There was a strange look on Bailey's face now. Pain was mixed with some other emotion that Anna didn't understand. "He admitted it to me."

"And you didn't *say* anything?"

Bailey's dark eyes connected with Anna's for a long second of silence before she answered. "No. I didn't. And that's all I'm going to say about it, Anna. I'm sorry. If you want the rest of the story, you'll have to ask Hoyt."

"I just can't believe he never *told* me." Anna could still remember the sense of betrayal and disbelief she'd felt when she'd been confronted about the discovery. The assistant principal had made it clear that Hoyt wasn't explicitly denying his own guilt. And Hoyt certainly hadn't come across as innocent during the hurried conversation she'd wrangled with him in the school stairwell.

He'd avoided her eyes, and there had been a mulish set to his jaw. He'd told her nothing apart from the fact that he was sorry and that she shouldn't worry. He'd make it clear to the assistant principal that she'd had nothing to do with the theft.

She'd pulled out all the stops, blasting him for jeopardizing both their hard-earned scholarships with such a stupid stunt. He'd just listened silently, apologized again and left her nursing a grudge that would last for more than a decade.

Now Bailey was telling her Hoyt hadn't even *done* it?

She set her half-eaten pizza down on the plate. "You know, Bailey, I'm a little tired. I think I'm going to call it a night and head on home."

Bailey drew in a deep, slow breath, but she didn't protest. "All right. We'll talk soon about setting up that cross-promotion. When you see Hoyt, tell him Jess will be fine with me until you guys are done hashing all this out."

"But I won't see Hoyt again tonight, Bailey."

The tiniest glimmer of a smile twinkled around Bailey's lips. "Just give him the message, Anna. Okay?"

As Anna left the store, she hesitated for a second in the shade of Bailey's crisp, green-striped awnings. Then she turned in the opposite direction of the bookstore.

It was still light out, and the day was cooling off. Maybe she'd take a walk around town.

She'd been thinking that she didn't get enough exercise, and Tino's pizza wasn't exactly diet food. A brisk walk would clear her head.

And, just in case Bailey was right, Anna would be safely away from Pages until Hoyt gave up and went home.

It was a good idea. It just didn't work. She made it exactly six steps before she heard a truck rumbling to a stop behind her.

"Anna?"

Anna didn't turn around, but her spine straightened and she picked up her pace, striding briskly away from him. "Hoyt, I'm really not in the mood for a conversation right now. I'm going for a walk." As she spoke, her high heel caught on the cracked sidewalk, making her wobble.

He winced. A walk? In those sandals? The old sidewalks were pretty dicey here. She was going to twist an ankle if she wasn't careful.

He hurried to catch up with her. It wasn't as easy as he'd thought. In spite of those silly shoes, Anna was logging some impressive mileage.

When he finally came up beside her, she wouldn't look at him.

"I don't blame you for being mad, Anna. Trust me, I'm mad myself. The guys—"

"I told you, I don't want to talk about it." She stumbled again, and he caught her elbow to steady her.

"Careful there. Are you sure a walk is a great idea? Those shoes and these messed-up sidewalks aren't a good combo, and it's starting to get dark. Let me drive you back to the store. It's a short ride." He paused and tried a smile. "Besides, you know you're dying to tell me off. There's no better place for that than the cab of a truck. I'll have nowhere to hide. Come on. What do you say?"

Anna hesitated, her lips pressed together in a tight line. "Oh, all *right*. But only because I'm about to break my neck trying to walk in these stupid things. I don't know why I ever bought them in the first place."

Hoyt glanced down at Anna's feet. The flimsy sandals sported tiny gold bangles sewn along the leather straps, and they had a toothpicky heel that looked like it would snap off if you looked at it too hard. And—surprisingly—the small toes peeking out of them were tipped with glossy rose.

Had he ever seen Anna wearing nail polish before? He didn't think so. His mind flashed back to the fancy hairdo he'd wrecked in front of Tino's. Anna had put some serious effort into upgrading her looks for the dinner tonight.

Somehow that made his heart go all tight and sore.

"They're pretty shoes. Just not so great for walking, maybe."

"And I definitely can't afford a trip to the emergency room." She picked her way back toward his truck. Hoyt stayed close, ready to shoot out an arm and catch her again if she looked like she was about to take a tumble.

Once they were in the truck, he started the engine and pulled away from the curb. He said a thankful prayer for the one-way streets around Pine Valley's town square. Having to go all the way around the block would buy him a few extra minutes. He had a feeling he was going to need every single one of them.

"Anna, I'm really sorry about what happened back at Tino's. I never—"

"You lied to me about stealing those test answers back in high school."

"What?" Hoyt darted a quick look at Anna. Where had that come from? He'd been all geared up to apologize for dragging her to Tino's to meet up with the Three Stooges. That was what he'd rehearsed the whole drive back from the restaurant.

He wasn't prepared to talk about this.

"Don't deny it. Maybe you didn't actually say the words, but you deliberately let me believe something that wasn't true."

He took his eyes off the road long enough to shoot a second bewildered glance in her direction. Anna was frowning at him, her green eyes sharp and accusing.

"If you didn't steal those answer keys, Hoyt, who did?" When he didn't answer right away, she lifted an eyebrow. "What difference does it make now if you tell me?"

That was exactly his question.

Well, one thing was for sure. This wasn't a conversation he needed to have while he was trying to drive, not even poking along like he was right now. He pulled the truck over in front of the church coffee shop and moved the gearshift into Park. Then he turned in the seat and faced Anna.

Okay, fine. If she really wanted to know the truth, he'd tell her.

"Danny Whitlock stole them. The guy was a genius with a lockpick."

"Danny?" Anna's brow furrowed as she thought that through. "Abel Whitlock's younger brother?"

"Yeah." He waited as she searched her memory, putting pieces together.

"I remember Danny being kind of a troublemaker, but why would he even want them? They weren't for any of his classes."

"He was planning to sell them."

He didn't offer any more of an explanation about that part of it. He didn't figure he needed to. Everybody had known that the Whitlock family had lived close to the bone. Money had been hard to come by, and only Abel had ever believed in getting it honestly.

He waited for Anna's next question. It wasn't long coming.

"Why did you take the blame? Covering for Danny cost you your scholarship, Hoyt! And if I'm remembering right, you didn't even like him all that much. Why on earth would you do such a thing?"

This was where things got tricky. He'd never told anybody the rest of this story. He'd never intended to.

But he was going to tell it now. Because somehow, in spite of all his arguments about how long ago this had all been, he wanted Anna to know the truth.

"Dan Whitlock's dad was tough to handle when he'd been drinking."

"I knew that." Anna's response was immediate. "Everybody knew that." She paused, and he could see her weighing her words. She finally took the plunge. "So was yours."

"Yeah, well." Hoyt shrugged. "I was a lot bigger than Danny. By the time I was a senior in high school, I could hold my own with my old man." Mostly. It depended on what impromptu weapon his enraged father happened to pick up. "Danny was better at getting in trouble than he was at defending himself. Besides, my father didn't care two beans about school. If I screwed up on the football field, sure. I was in for it. But the rest of the time, school wasn't even on my father's radar."

He hoped Anna wouldn't look too closely at that particular argument. The football scholarship to UGA had definitely been on his father's radar, and Hoyt had gotten the beating of his life when his hungover dad had blearily clued in on the fact that he wouldn't be bragging down at the bar anymore about his son playing college ball.

"I had less to lose. Besides, Dan was one of the guys on my team. It was my job to look after him, if I could."

"You had less to lose? You can't be serious. That was a *full-ride* scholarship you threw away, Hoyt! To the University of Georgia." He could see that Anna was gearing up to bluster at him about how wonderful a college education was and what a golden opportunity he'd blown. He'd heard it all before, and he didn't have the time to listen to it all again now. He cut her off.

"I was never going to go anyway. I had to put food on my mother's table, Anna. I had to run the construction business. My father's drinking was off the charts by then, and there was no way he could have done it without me. If I'd gone to Athens, Mom would have been all alone. She'd have starved. If Dad didn't beat her to death first."

Anna's eyes widened, and Hoyt winced. He probably shouldn't have been so blunt. There was a good bit of innocence mixed in with Anna Delaney's spunk; there always had been.

"Why didn't you tell me it was Danny who stole the tests, Hoyt? I guess I can see why you did…what you did. But I don't understand why you didn't just tell me the truth."

Because you never would have stood for it. Everything was so black-and-white to you…you never could see all the shades of gray I had to deal with.

"I guess I didn't think you needed to know."

"But Bailey Quinn needed to know?"

"I didn't tell Bailey." He paused. "But yeah. She probably did need to know. She and Danny—" He cut himself off. "I didn't tell her."

"Who *did* you tell?" Anna was watching him intently as she waited for his answer. The woman should have been a lawyer. She could pin you down like nobody he'd ever seen.

"I told the people who *did* need to know. The seniors on the football team who'd planned on buying the keys from Danny. I let them have it, I'll tell you that. And then I told them I'd take care of it as best I could. I didn't mean any insult by not telling you. I just knew it would put you in a hard spot, knowing the truth. Your dad being the principal and all. I figured you'd have felt like you had to tell him, and you wouldn't have understood what was at stake. You came from a whole different world than Danny and I did."

"A different world." She spoke so quietly that he had

to bend closer to catch what she was saying. It was as if she'd forgotten he was even in the truck and was talking to herself. "I guess maybe you're right." She considered him silently for a second or two. "You know what? I wish I had been the kind of person you could have told back then, Hoyt. I really do."

He didn't know quite how to answer that. He cleared his throat and glanced at his watch. "I'd better drive you home. It'll be Jess's bedtime pretty soon, and Mitch is probably wondering what happened to us." And waiting to help set up the surprise Hoyt was planning for Anna. Of course, after everything that had happened tonight, there was no telling how that would turn out.

Anna blinked several times and then nodded. "I'd forgotten Mitch was waiting at the store. You're right. We should go."

They didn't talk for the rest of the short drive. At first, Hoyt tried to think of something to say, something that might bridge over the gap that had opened up between them. But Anna stared out her window, her face blank. She didn't seem to want to talk, so in the end, Hoyt just let things be.

When they pulled up, the bookstore lights were gleaming, and he could see Mitch hunched over the checkout counter scribbling some notes on the pocket-size notepad he always carried. The electrical contractor looked up when the door opened.

"There you two are. I was just finishing up." He smiled, but his eyes cut over to Hoyt's, telegraphing a message that made a prickle run up Hoyt's backbone.

He'd worked with Mitch for years, and he knew that look. It always meant the same thing.

Bad news.

"Smoke alarm installed?" Hoyt kept his voice casual.

"You better believe it." Mitch turned to Anna, and his expression gentled. "I've installed three, and they're the best we have. They react to both heat and smoke, and they'll call the fire department for you if they go off. You'll be perfectly safe until we get the wiring repaired."

Hoyt could read the warning beneath Mitch's reassurances, but Anna didn't seem to pick up on it. She set her purse down on the top of a handy bookshelf and took a deep breath.

"Thank you very much. So, now that you've looked around, what do you think, Mr. Connor? How much will it cost to get the building up to code?"

"First of all, please call me Mitch. We're all friends here." His gaze flitted briefly to Hoyt's and then back to Anna. "And I'm sorry, but I don't know the answer to that yet. I have to price the material and do some figuring."

Anna's shoulders relaxed. "Of course. I should have realized. Will you call me when you've worked it out?"

Mitch's gaze never once flicked in Hoyt's direction. "I never like to have meetings over the phone. Why don't you come to my house for dinner this Friday night, you and Hoyt, and we'll talk it all through? Chloe—my wife—is a fabulous cook, and I think she'd really enjoy meeting you."

The man was smooth. If Hoyt hadn't been in on the plan he'd never have taken it for anything other than a spur-of-the-moment invitation.

Anna didn't seem to suspect anything, although he could see she was a little taken aback by being asked to visit the home of someone she barely knew.

"We really do need to get this all worked out as soon as possible," Hoyt pointed out quickly. "Friday's good for me. What about you, Anna? Are you free for supper on Friday?"

Anna hesitated. Then, to Hoyt's relief, she nodded at Mitch. "All right. Thank you. If you're sure it wouldn't be too much trouble."

"No trouble at all." Mitch flipped his notebook closed and shoved it down in the pocket of his dark blue jeans. "Hoyt, I'll walk out with you. I have a question about the wiring for the medical annex." The electrical contractor nodded again at Anna. "Chloe and I will look forward to seeing you Friday, Anna."

When they were safely out on the sidewalk, Hoyt shot a sideways glance at his friend.

"How bad is it?"

"Bad." Mitch ran one hand through his hair. "You were smart to insist on the fire alarms. I wouldn't want my worst enemy sleeping in that building."

That was what he'd been afraid of. Well, rats. "It'll be expensive then."

Mitch shrugged. "It's going to take a lot of material. The labor's no problem. I can give you that for nothing, as long as it doesn't interfere with our paying jobs."

They were talking about a lot of work. Hoyt shook his head. "Nobody expects you to donate your time, Mitch."

"I'm glad to do it." Mitch halted at his truck, one hand on the door handle. "I'm not blind, Hoyt. I see how you look at Anna." The easy smile faded from the electrician's face, and he reached out one hand to clench Hoyt's forearm in a brief, hard clasp. "And you're sure going to a lot of trouble to make her happy. It's obvious you care a lot about this girl. So you're both welcome to whatever help I can give." Mitch shot a careful look back toward the bookstore and lowered his voice. "By the way, I wasn't lying when I said Chloe would be glad to see Anna. Chloe's about ready to wring your neck over that little surprise of yours."

Uh-oh. He'd better send Chloe some flowers. "Sorry about that."

"Nah, don't worry about it. It's worth it to see that gooey look on your face again, man. Chloe and I are really happy for you both."

Hoyt shook his head. "You're reading way too much into this, Mitch. It's not like that."

"No?" Mitch chuckled as he opened the door of his truck. "Not yet, maybe. We'll see what happens on Friday."

Chapter Ten

"Owls have three eyeballs!" Jess announced from her booster seat as they drove to the Connor home on Friday evening.

Hoyt exchanged an amused glance with Anna. "I think you mean *eyelids*, baby." Today had been all about owls at preschool, and Jess had been talking birds non-stop since she got home.

Probably because she hadn't spoken to anybody else all day. Jess still wasn't talking to anybody other than him and Anna, and in spite of Jacob Stone's warning, some troubling what-ifs were niggling around in the back of Hoyt's mind.

The truck tire slammed hard into a pothole. "Sorry, ladies. I should've been watching out for that one. This road is rough."

"Owls swallow their food whole!" Jess was wearing a lopsided construction-paper owl mask over her face so her words were muffled.

But they were still words. Beautiful, perfectly un-derstandable words, and although he'd already pretty much had his fill of owl trivia for the day, he'd never get tired of hearing Jess's voice.

He needed to do what Jacob had suggested. Focus on his blessings and leave outcomes in the hands of the Lord.

"I have a great book about owls back at the store, sweetie." Anna had one arm draped over the seat and was smiling back at Jess. "It has wonderful photographs in it and lots of interesting facts. Maybe we could read it together."

Jess hooted approvingly and kicked her tiny feet against the base of her seat. Anna laughed and hooted back. There was an affectionate sparkle in her green eyes as she listened to Jess's chatter. The endless parade of owl facts didn't seem to bug Anna at all.

In fact, she seemed downright fascinated. He didn't think Anna had given him more than a quick glance since she'd climbed into the truck.

That was bugging *him* just a little bit, and he found himself wishing she'd throw a few of those smiles in his direction.

Come on. Was he actually feeling jealous here over the attention Anna was showering on Jess? Because that was just…ridiculous.

His feelings for Anna had been all over the map lately, sure. But that was because of how much she'd helped Jess. He was grateful.

At least that's what he'd been telling himself.

What had Mitch said? *I see how you look at Anna.* Hoyt shifted on the truck seat. Connor was just putting stupid ideas in his head. He and Anna were friends. Really good friends. At least he hoped they were. But that was all.

He wasn't looking for anything else.

He'd only dated once since Marylee's death, and it hadn't gone well. The whole night he'd felt so uncomfortable that he'd never even considered trying it again.

But now, hearing Anna's soft laugh, watching her gently prodding Jess to speak more, seeing how her face lit up when she really smiled…

This didn't feel uncomfortable at all. It felt *right* to him, relaxing and familiar, the way a man felt when he finally made it safely home at the end of a long day.

Then again there was that spice of unexpectedness to Anna that kept him on his toes. He liked that about her.

He liked that a lot.

Hoyt stared through the smudged windshield, but he wasn't really seeing the road in front of him. Did all these feelings he'd been having about Anna really just boil down to gratitude? Or was Mitch onto something?

"Daddy!" Jess stopped hooting long enough to mount a protest. "You're going past the gate to Uncle Mitch's!"

Lost in his thoughts, Hoyt had missed the turn into the Connors' gated driveway. When Jess spoke, he stepped on the brake and geared down automatically in order to reverse, but his mind wasn't on what he was doing. He turned to look at his daughter.

Uncle Mitch. Mitch had given himself that honorary title as soon as he'd met Jess, but Hoyt hadn't heard those once-familiar words come out of his daughter's mouth in years.

"Uncle Mitch is a 'lectrician," Jess informed Anna cheerfully. "And Aunt Chloe teaches fifth grade. I *love* them, and I love their whole big family. And Aunt Chloe makes the best food in the world. You're going to love them all, too, Miss Anna!"

"I'm sure I will!" Anna's voice was still bright, but now her enthusiasm sounded as fake as the owl tattoo on Jess's arm. "So, the Connors have a lot of children?"

"They have four. All boys." He paused, but he knew Anna might as well be prepared. "But Mitch has three brothers living within driving distance who also have kids, and they're a close family. There might be a crowd."

Hoyt put the truck back in first gear and turned down the rutted road that led to a simple metal farm gate. He stole a look at Anna's face as he stopped the truck. Just like he'd figured. The relaxed smile he'd been admiring had vanished the minute he'd said the word *crowd.* Hoyt felt a prickle of uncertainty.

He'd been so intent on setting up his surprise for Anna that he'd forgotten something about the Connors. To Mitch and Chloe, anything fewer than forty people was just another family dinner.

It would be fine, he reassured himself. The Connors, all of them, were the warmest and friendliest people Hoyt knew, and Jess was right. Chloe's cooking outclassed that of any restaurant in a fifty-mile radius of Pine Valley. They'd set Anna at ease in no time, and Hoyt's secret make-Anna-happy plan would be a roaring success.

At least, he hoped so. He sure didn't want his newest bright idea to backfire like the airplane ride had.

Please, Lord. Help a guy out here.

"Hoyt? Is something wrong? Why are we just sitting still?" Anna was looking at him, one dark eyebrow raised.

Hoyt refocused. "Hang on just a second. I have to open the gate. The Connors have cows in this pasture."

"Moos!" Jess announced happily from the back seat. "I love moos *and* owls!"

"I'll open it." Anna hopped out before he could argue. He watched her unhook the chain on the gate, then his gaze skimmed over to where the Connors' brick home sat on the crest of the hill. He counted at least three extra vehicles. The Connors had turned out in full force to witness the surprise he was about to spring on Anna.

Oh, brother.

What was that other thing Mitch had said?

We'll see what happens on Friday.

They'd see, all right. One way or the other, things were definitely about to get interesting.

Anna was ready to run back to the car before she even made it to the door of the two-story brick home. She'd expected a quiet dinner, and she'd been nervous enough about that. This was shaping up to be something altogether different. Several cars were parked around the house, and at least half a dozen children were swarming around the shaded yard, chasing each other and screaming with glee.

As they reached the semicircular steps leading up to the porch, a small, sturdy boy jogged in their direction. He was looking over his shoulder and laughing, his attention focused on the two bigger girls who were pursuing him. Just when he was about to mow Jess flat, Hoyt stepped in front of his daughter and caught the boy midstride, swinging the little fellow up in his arm.

"Careful there, kiddo!"

"Uncle Hoyt! You're finally here! Boy, is Mom going

to be glad to see you! You're in big trouble. He keeps getting out, and he chewed a hole in the—"

"Sh!" One of the bigger girls spoke up as she skidded to a stop. "That's a secret, Logan! You're not supposed to talk about it!"

A worried look creased the boy's face as he looked at Anna. "Oops. Sorry, Uncle Hoyt. Hey, Jess. We're playing tag. Come on!" He grabbed Jess's hand, and the children ran off together toward a huge oak tree that seemed to be functioning as home base.

Anna looked up at Hoyt. He was smiling as he watched his owl-masked daughter joining in the game. "What was that all about?"

Hoyt suddenly looked evasive. "Nothing much." Ignoring the doorbell, he eased the large oak door open a crack. "Chloe? We're here."

"In the kitchen, Hoyt!" a woman's voice called back. "Come on in."

They stepped inside a cool entryway with a gleaming wooden floor and a jumble of family pictures crowding the cream-colored walls. Through an arched entryway to her right Anna could see a living room decorated in cozy shades of rust and pumpkin, where several people were intent on a baseball game playing on a flat-screen television. Something important must have happened because the group erupted into loud cheers and started high-fiving each other.

The decibel level was off the charts, and Anna fought the urge to clap her hands over her ears. How many people were in this house?

"Come on." Hoyt put a reassuring hand on the small of her back, ushering her past the polished staircase hugging the wall. Anna's nerves were jumping like raindrops hitting a puddle, but she could still feel every one of the warm, strong fingers against the base of her spine. "Trust me. You're going to love Chloe."

Whing! Something whizzed past Anna's shoulder. Before Hoyt could react, the sound of a rapid-fire Nerf gun came from the railing overlooking the foyer. *Blat! Blat-blat-blat-blat-blat!*

A shower of yellow foam projectiles rained upon the two of them, bouncing off their bodies. Hoyt stepped in front of Anna. "Whoa! Cease fire!"

"What's going on out here?" A tall woman hurried through an arched doorway in the back of the foyer. Her long, dark hair was twisted on top of her head with the kind of casual elegance Anna could never manage to pull off, and she held her floury hands in front of a big white apron. "Noah! Liam! What are you *doing*? Inanimate targets only, remember? And we certainly don't shoot at our guests!"

Hoyt looked sheepish. "Go easy on them, Chloe. This is my fault. Last time I was here, I ambushed them in the backyard with the water hose, remember? They're just paying me back."

"I'm so sorry." Chloe turned to Anna. Her tone was serious, but there was an affectionate maternal twinkle in her dark eyes. She shot a narrow glance at Hoyt. "Apparently my sons have come under some questionable influences. Come here, boys, and apologize to Miss Anna."

Two sheepish boys clumped down the steps, oversize plastic weaponry drooping in their hands. They shot guilty glances at each other as they approached.

The two culprits looked to be between six and eight

years old. They were obviously brothers and as cute as buttons.

"Sorry if we scared you." The taller one spoke up first. "We didn't mean to. We was just playing."

"Were." Both Anna and Chloe made the automatic correction at the same time. The two women glanced at each other, startled. Anna flushed, wishing she could find some hole to crawl into.

The stupid correction had bypassed her good manners and jumped right past her lips. She hadn't even been in the house five minutes, and she'd already offended her hostess. This was a new record.

But to Anna's astonishment, Chloe only threw back her head and laughed. "Finally! Somebody else who won't stand for sloppy grammar. The good Lord knew I needed reinforcements. You and I are going to get along just fine. Hoyt, I'm covered with flour. Take charge of those guns for me, will you? Just put them on top of that bookcase over there. No," Chloe cut sharp eyes at her sons as they started to protest. "You knew the rules. No arguments or it'll be that much longer before you get them back."

Hoyt held out his hands for the toys, and, groaning, the two boys surrendered them. "Sorry, guys. What can I say? You know your mom's the boss of me."

Chloe chuckled again. "I'm the boss of everybody around here, and don't any of you forget it." She reached out with both hands and touched the tips of her sons' noses, dusting them lightly with flour. "Now go play outside with your cousins and leave the house in peace. Anna, I need to get back to my biscuits. Would you like to come back to the kitchen with me, or would you rather watch baseball with the others?"

"I'm not really that into sports," Anna confessed.

"Wonderful!" A friendly smile warmed Chloe's face. "I was hoping you'd say that. I love having company in the kitchen."

"You might have more of that if you didn't always put people to work back there!" called a female voice from the living room. "Take my advice, new person. Come watch baseball with us, or she'll have you up to your elbows in whatever she's cooking back there."

"My sister-in-law is a very funny woman." Chloe raised her voice to be heard over the noise of the game. "But she's also going to be a very hungry woman if she doesn't stay on my good side."

"Hey, I brought a pecan pie, didn't I?" the other woman pointed out. "And ice cream. I did my part."

"I'll come back to the kitchen with Anna," Hoyt said. "I could use another biscuit-making lesson anyway. The last time I tried your recipe, the things came out like hockey pucks."

"You handled the dough too much then. I told you that makes them tough. But I don't have time to give you pointers right now." Chloe turned to the side and gave Hoyt a playful push with one narrow shoulder. "Tell you what. You love watching the Braves. Why don't you go on and watch the game with Mitch and let me get acquainted with Anna here?"

Hoyt shot Anna an uncertain glance. "That all right with you?"

"Of course." Anna spoke with more confidence than she felt.

Hoyt hesitated for another second and then nodded. "Okay, then." He set the confiscated toys on top of the bookshelf, smiled again at Anna and headed in the direction of the living room.

You'll be fine, that smile seemed to say.

She wished she believed that.

Chloe watched him go, an affectionate smile lingering on her lips. Then she turned to Anna and tilted her head. "The kitchen's back this way. I love your blouse, by the way. Such a pretty shade of green."

"Thanks." As Anna followed her down the short hallway, she caught a glimpse of the outfit the other woman's huge chef's apron was concealing. Chloe was wearing a black dress patterned with large, vibrantly red poppies. Cut just above her knees, the artistically uneven hemline fluttered as she moved gracefully down the narrow space.

Suddenly feeling woefully underdressed, Anna smoothed her khaki slacks and tugged her carefully ironed linen shirt a bit straighter as they stepped into the kitchen.

Unlike Anna's shabby galley kitchen, this room looked like something out of a magazine. Every single feature looked well crafted and pricey. The floor was tiled in ruddy rectangles, and the cabinets were a dark cream. A huge stainless steel stove was angled under a brick arch on the far wall, and a generous island split the space in half and provided an ample workspace.

It was all beautiful, but the space obviously wasn't just for show. The air was thick with appetizing scents, and a gleaming pot on the stove had dribbles of a rich red sauce snaking down its side. On the white-sprinkled island was a metal bowl holding a heaping mound of flour.

Chloe moved to the small, deep sink at one end of

the island and washed her hands. "At the risk of proving Donna right, I really could use some help if you're up for it."

"Of course." Anna moved to the sink. "I should warn you, though. I've never been very good at biscuits. Mine would probably make Hoyt's hockey pucks taste good."

Chloe laughed. "Oh, don't you worry. I always use my grandmother's recipe, and Hoyt notwithstanding, it's foolproof. Her buttermilk biscuits melt in your mouth. If you work the shortening in with your fingers and don't overhandle the dough they turn out perfectly every single time. I'll show you."

Anna quickly washed and dried her hands. Following Chloe's instructions, she began to work the blob of vegetable shortening into the silky flour.

"Just keep rubbing it in until it's like little crumbs," Chloe said. She was busying herself with a dark, leafy salad at the other end of the island. "My mother always cut the shortening in with two knives, but I do better when I can feel the texture with my hands." For the next minute or two, they chatted about cooking, and Anna started to relax. "There, that's perfect. Now we add in the liquids." Chloe left the salad to snag a carton of buttermilk from the refrigerator and set it by Anna's elbow. "You can do the honors."

Anna unscrewed the plastic cap on the container. "How much?"

"Gram would say 'until it looks right.'" Chloe chuckled at Anna's doubtful expression. "I know. But Gram believed the best cooks never measure anything. They just add a dash and a dribble of this or that until the dish turns out like they want it to. Basically, you want all the dough to gather together. That's it. Now, we'll have to handle it lightly as we roll it out and cut it." Chloe tossed more flour on her work surface and dumped out the mound of dough. "This is the part Hoyt messes up. He's too heavy-handed. Tell you what, I'll show you, and you can save me the trouble of giving him a refresher lesson."

Chloe obviously had the wrong idea. Anna shook her head. "I'm not sure I'd ever have the opportunity. Hoyt and I don't usually— We're just friends."

A smile tugged up the corners of the other woman's mouth. "Oh? Well, friends cook together sometimes, don't they? Like you and I are doing now. Careful, there. Put a tiny bit more flour on your rolling pin. The dough's sticking. Now you've got it. So you and Hoyt aren't dating?"

Well, Chloe Connor certainly didn't pull any punches. Anna refloured the wooden pin meticulously, avoiding the other woman's eyes.

"No, we're not. There. Do I have this rolled thin enough?"

"Yes. It's perfect. Here." Chloe handed her a glass tumbler. "Gram always used the rim of a tea glass to cut out her biscuits—so I do, too. I have tons of metal cutters, but doing it this way reminds me of her. Dip it in the flour first." There was a short awkward pause before Chloe spoke again. "Hoyt's a great guy, you know. A fantastic dad, too. I know he can come across a little rough around the edges sometimes, but deep down where it counts he's an absolute jewel."

"Mmm." Anna didn't quite know what to say to that. She transferred circles of biscuit dough onto the waiting baking sheet with suddenly clumsy fingers. "Does the oven need to be preheated for these?"

"Yes. I've already switched it on, and it's nice and hot." Suddenly Chloe reached around Anna's shoulders and gave her a brief, hard hug. "Now I've made you uncomfortable. I'm so sorry, Anna. I shouldn't be poking into your personal business like this. Hoyt and Jess just have a very special place in our hearts, that's all. And you're the first woman he's ever brought out here to meet us. He's been going on and on about how wonderful you are, so I just assumed— Never mind. If you'll forgive me, I promise I'll behave myself."

Anna smiled and nodded, but her knees suddenly felt wobbly. Hoyt had called her wonderful? Really?

Suddenly, there was a chorus of shouts from the front of the house, followed by a rapid skittering sound. Chloe tensed and turned toward the doorway with an expression of horror. "Mitch? That better not be what I think it is!"

A small brown-and-white dog barreled into the kitchen, followed hard by Mitch and Hoyt. The animal skidded across the gleaming tiles, tongue lolling, looking well pleased with himself.

The two men stopped in the doorway. They didn't look pleased at all.

"I'm sorry, Chloe. He got out of his crate somehow, and you know he doesn't pay much attention when he's called."

"That's because he's a very *naughty* dog who doesn't behave himself!" Chloe leveled a stern look at the furry offender. He yipped back sassily, and Anna laughed. Apparently Chloe's no-nonsense tone worked better on adorable little boys than on adorable little dogs.

And the dog *was* darling. Anna crouched down and wiggled hopeful fingers in the puppy's direction. He advanced a few cautious steps and sniffed her, his tail wagging slowly. "Aww, but who could be mad at that face? He's so cute." Anna laughed as the dog licked her hand. "And I just can't get over how much he looks like a stuffed dog I used to have when I was a little girl. Doesn't he, Hoyt? Isn't it amazing?" She fondled the soft, floppy ears.

He liked being petted. He butted his round little head up into her palm enthusiastically. Anna was so caught up with the dog that it took her a second or two to realize that the room had gone strangely silent.

She glanced up to find everybody looking at Hoyt.

"Sorry, Hoyt." Chloe made a rueful face. "It looks like the cat's out of the bag. Or the dog's out of the crate. Whatever. Either way, the secret's out now. You might as well go ahead and tell her."

For once Hoyt looked oddly unsure of himself. His cheeks were the exact same ruddy red of the tiled floor, and he was shifting his weight from one boot to the other.

"Hoyt?" Anna frowned. "What's Chloe talking about? What's going on?"

"Surprise," Hoyt said quietly. "He's yours."

"Mine? I—don't understand." Anna looked down at the happy animal who was trying his best to climb into her lap. "You—got me a dog?"

Mitch laughed. "Not *a* dog. *The* dog. It's no accident he looks so much like your toy. Hoyt searched every shelter database within driving distance until he found one that looked just like that."

"He's a rescue from two counties over," Hoyt volunteered sheepishly. "Chloe's been fostering him until you could pick him up. I have dog food and a bed and everything he needs. And he's already been checked out by a vet, and he got a clean bill of health."

"He's certainly full of energy. You're going to have your work cut out for you when you start training him," Chloe spoke up wryly. "He chews on everything, and he's stubborn as a mule."

Anna didn't answer. She couldn't quite form words, and the world had gone a little blurry.

"I hope this is okay," Hoyt said. "I guess maybe I should have cleared this with you first, but I wanted it to be a surprise."

"I'm so sorry." Somehow Anna forced the words past the lump in her throat. She could feel everybody's eyes on her, and suddenly it was all too much. "Could you all excuse me for a minute, please?" Blindly, she headed for the back door, pushing through it into the heat of the late Georgia afternoon.

Chapter Eleven

"Sure, genius. Give the woman a dog that reminds her of the biggest lie her father ever told her. *Stupid* idea," Hoyt muttered as he went out the back door in search of Anna. At Chloe's insistence, he'd waited before following her.

"She probably just needs a few moments by herself, Hoyt."

He hoped Chloe was right, but he was pretty sure he'd just made another huge mistake. Apparently, when it came to Anna's feelings, he had all the finesse of a silverback gorilla turned loose in a room full of breakables.

"Stupid," he muttered again.

Anna was standing under a trio of pines in the corner of the yard, looking out over the Connors' back pasture. Hoyt made his way over to her, his brain fumbling for something halfway decent to say.

She had her back to him, but she was standing on a thick carpet of crunchy pine needles, so there was no way to make his approach quiet. He could tell the instant she knew he was there, because her shoulders stiffened.

He halted a few steps behind her.

"You don't have to keep the dog. I'll find him another home." He might as well get the rest of this over with while she was already ticked off with him. "The Connors had nothing to do with this, by the way. This was all my idea. I asked Mitch to invite you over here so I could give you the puppy, not to talk about the electrical repairs for your store. Mitch and I are going to take care of those. I'm donating the material, and the work won't cost you a cent."

She turned to face him, and his heart fell. Her face was splotchy, and her eyes were red-rimmed. He'd made her cry with his dumb dog surprise.

Chalk up another disaster for the gorilla.

"I'm sorry, Anna. This was a bad idea. I really didn't mean to upset you."

She waved her hand, and he could see her slim throat working as she tried to get words out. "Hoyt," she whispered finally.

He hurried to make his case. "I think I know what you're going to say. You don't want me to do the repairs, and I don't blame you. But please let me help you out. It's important to me to pay you back somehow for what you're doing for Jess. Not many people have ever…gone out of their way for me. You have, and I'm not just talking about now, with Jess. You did back in high school, too. Somehow I keep messing things up between us, so you'd probably be better off just letting me handle your repairs for you. I'm good at that kind of stuff." He attempted a laugh. "Otherwise who knows what kind of crazy stunt I might try next? Just be glad your dad didn't give you a stuffed elephant." She didn't laugh. Okay, too soon to joke about this. "Like I said, I'm sorry. Believe it or not, I'm trying to get this right. I really am."

"You did."

She spoke so shakily he wasn't sure he'd heard her right. "What?"

"You did get it right, Hoyt. That little dog." Her voice broke again. "I can promise you, he's not going home with anybody but me. He's...he's just *perfect.* And you went to all that trouble... That's the sweetest, kindest thing anybody's ever done for me." A fat tear rolled down her cheek, and she sniffed and shook her head and tried to laugh. "I'm the one who's sorry. No wonder you got the wrong idea—me running out here like that. I just didn't want everybody to see me blubbering like a baby." She swiped at her cheek with the back of one hand and sniffled.

Relief swamped him so completely that for a moment his knees actually sagged. Anna was crying because she was *happy.*

He shoved a hand in his jeans pocket and yanked out a ragged handkerchief. It was one of the first things he'd learned the hard way in Single Dad 101. Always carry something to wipe tears and noses with. He stepped forward, intending to offer it to Anna.

That was what he planned to do. But instead, for a reason he could never put his finger on afterward, he didn't do that. He used the wadded cloth to gently wipe her tears away himself.

As he did, his eyes locked onto her shimmering green ones, and all the memories and worries he'd been juggling faded into a dim blur. The only thing left to focus on was this moment, the one he was standing in with Anna.

He leaned forward, closer than he'd ever been to her, and hesitated, just for a second. Then something deep inside him snapped loose, and he crossed the last gap standing between himself and complete insanity.

He kissed Anna Delaney.

He couldn't believe this was happening. Somewhere in the farthest corner of his brain, his last functioning brain cells were shooting up warning flares like crazy.

He couldn't have cared less.

"Hoyt!"

Mitch's urgent call coming from the direction of the Connors' kitchen had the effect of a shrilling alarm pulling him out of a dream. Hoyt broke the kiss and drew back. Anna's eyes fluttered dazedly open, and she stumbled backward across the crunchy needles, her cheeks flaming.

"Hoyt, come here!" He glanced over to see Mitch beckoning from the kitchen door. *"Hurry!"*

Anna looked like she'd had the wind knocked out of her. He couldn't understand much about what had just happened, but he understood that. He felt the same way.

He'd just *kissed* her. This was huge. So huge, in fact, that he was kind of amazed that the world was still right side up.

"Anna." Her name came out hoarse and uncertain. Then he stopped because he had absolutely no idea what he was supposed to say at this point. "I—"

"You'd better go see what he wants." Anna's voice didn't sound any too steady, either.

"I guess so." Hoyt hesitated for another awkward second before turning toward the house. The minute he did, the thinking part of his brain jolted back awake and started buzzing like a freshly charged power drill.

What did you just do, you idiot?

"Hoyt." Mitch had walked out into the yard to meet him. "Sorry. I didn't mean to interrupt—whatever it was I interrupted. But this is…well, it's important."

Chloe zipped by them, sparing her husband one quick, disapproving glance. "You could have waited five seconds longer," she murmured before lifting her voice. "Anna? Come back inside. Mitch is right, although his timing stinks. This is important."

"What is it?" Hoyt was having a hard time focusing. His brain had that kiss playing on some kind of loop.

What was Anna thinking right now?

A lot…maybe *everything*…depended on the answer to that question.

"You'd better come see for yourself." Mitch pushed him back into the kitchen.

Things seemed normal. Jess and three of the younger kids were on the floor, absorbed in a lively game of tug-of-war with the puppy.

The hair on the back of Hoyt's neck prickled. Calm, steady Mitch was shaking with excitement. Something big was up, and Hoyt sure hoped he'd guessed what it was.

He pushed the kiss to the back of his mind and leveled a don't-play-with-me look at his friend. "Mitch, what's going on?"

"Just hold on a second. And *listen*." Mitch raised his voice. "Jess? Honey? What's the puppy's name?"

Hoyt's overtaxed heart stammered to a complete halt, and his fingers clenched around the doorjamb. He zeroed in on his daughter and waited with everything he was worth.

Jess teasingly—and silently—wiggled the old sock the puppy had gripped in his teeth.

"Jess?" Mitch prompted gently.

Jess looked up from her game, gave an exaggerated sigh and rolled her eyes. "*Uncle Mitch!* I've *told* you and *told* you already. His *name* is *Chester*."

Hoyt's normally trustworthy knees surprised him by trying to buckle for the second time in one night.

"She's talking to me," Mitch murmured. "Chloe, too, and the kids. When my brothers are in the room, she gets quiet again. But this is still a big step forward, right?"

There was no way Hoyt was going to be able to answer around the wad of feelings stuck in his throat, so he just nodded.

Yeah. It was.

He crossed the room and picked up his daughter, squeezing her gently against his chest and murmuring words that didn't even make sense in her ear. So much for Dr. Mills's instructions not to make a big deal out of Jess's progress.

He didn't care. This *was* a big deal.

Anna was standing in the doorway, and when he caught her eye, she offered him a shaky smile. Chloe narrowed her eyes and shot a thoughtful glance between Anna and Hoyt. Then she looped one arm around Anna's waist and gave her a friendly squeeze.

"This is definitely a day for surprises, isn't it?"

Anna glanced at Hoyt, and the minute their eyes met, he was right back under those pine trees again.

Surprises didn't even begin to cover it.

At three thirty the following afternoon, Anna stood behind her checkout counter, a phone cradled against her shoulder. She was ringing up a sale for a customer and using one foot to nudge Chester away from the trash can he seemed intent on knocking over for the third time.

Anna mouthed a silent thank-you to the customer as she handed over his bag of books and then refocused her attention on the phone conversation. “Bobby, I really don’t think you should pay the full face value for the gift certificates. What about a twenty percent discount?” She listened, frowning. “Well, no. I wouldn’t want to mess up your accounting. Okay, if you say so. I’ll get them printed out and ready for you to pick up this afternoon.”

The bells on the door chimed just as she ended the call. She glanced up, her heart pounding. It wasn’t Hoyt, just a middle-aged couple who joined the other customers already browsing through her shelves.

She hadn’t had a Saturday this busy since…well, *ever.* She’d hardly found time to walk Chester, not that he was far enough along in his house training for that to matter very much. She had two books on puppy care sitting beside the cash register, and she planned to study them tonight. In the meantime, she’d carpeted the whole area behind the checkout counter with the disposable absorbent pads Chloe had handed her last night.

“I’ve tried to start training him for you, but your new buddy here has a head like a rock,” Chloe had warned her with a rueful smile.

Anna didn’t care. As far as she was concerned, Chester had no faults. Last night he’d whined in the crate Hoyt had provided, and Anna had used the excuse to unlatch the door and cuddle the puppy in her bed. They’d stayed that way all night, his cold little nose burrowed into her neck, his small warmth solid and comforting against her side.

No, Chester wasn't the one frustrating her today.

She'd been expecting Hoyt all day, but he hadn't come by yet. They hadn't had any opportunity to talk after…what had happened. Jess had chattered all the way home, while Chester filled in the gaps with morose howls from his carrier.

Hoyt had thrown her one long look as he'd pulled up in front of the store, but "I'll see you tomorrow" was all he'd said.

She'd stayed awake most of the night, stroking her snoring puppy and reliving that unbelievable kiss under the pine trees. She'd taken that moment apart and put it back together more times than she could count. Unfortunately, when morning had finally dawned, she'd been no closer to figuring it out.

She was no expert on kisses. She'd experienced embarrassingly few of them, as a matter of fact. But as far as she could tell, Hoyt had certainly kissed her like he'd meant it. She'd expected him to be banging on her door first thing this morning. And he definitely wouldn't catch her sporting crazy hair and yoga pants this time. She'd taken extra care with her clothes and her makeup, and she'd come downstairs with her squirming puppy half an hour before her regular time.

As the clock had ticked away the minutes, she'd learned something.

It was humiliating to have a handsome man show up unexpectedly when you were wearing your rattiest outfit and your hair looked like you hadn't brushed it in a month, true. But it was even more humiliating to fix yourself up for that man, expecting him to drop by after he'd surprised the life out of you by kissing you right out of the blue—and then have him not show up at all.

The door chimed again. Anna jerked her head up for the hundredth time that day, but again, it wasn't Hoyt. Instead, Chloe Connor walked into Pages, looking around herself as she adjusted a tangerine scarf she had flung over her shoulders. She caught sight of Anna, smiled and advanced with a purposeful step.

"Hi! I've finally found a minute to check out your bookstore. I haven't been in here two seconds, and I'm already kicking myself for not finding time to come in sooner! This place is charming."

She opened the clasps of the small purse that hung from her forearm and dug out a slip of paper. "Might as well jump right in. Here's a list of books I'd like you to order. I always spend part of the summer looking for new books to add to my classroom library. The school budget's really tight, so I usually just pay for them myself. Can you get them for me?"

"Of course." Anna scanned the elegant scrawl of writing. There were at least a dozen books listed. "You want *all* of these?"

"Absolutely. And I'm open to suggestions. If you know of any others I should take a look at, just let me know."

"I'm sure I can find some more for you to consider, and Pages offers a discount for educators. I'll get these ordered right away, and they'll probably be here in a week or so."

"Perfect. I'll have another list by then, probably." Chloe's brown eyes twinkled warmly. "I may as well warn you, I'm planning to be your very best customer. Although—" she glanced around the room, one eyebrow arched "—it looks like I'm going to have some stiff competition."

Anna smiled as she looked around her store. Most of the people milling around carried promising stacks of books in their arms, and she'd already processed more sales today than she had all last month. "Hoyt helped me set up some cross-promotions with local business owners. I was skeptical about it, but I have to say, it's made an amazing difference."

In more ways than one. Yes, the promotions Stork and Bobby were running were bringing new customers in. And earlier today, when Bailey Quinn had popped in during her lunch hour to brainstorm ideas about how Bailey's and Pages could work together, they'd come up with some really interesting possibilities.

Best of all, she and Bailey had laughed together as Chester growled his high-pitched puppy growl and tugged on Anna's sandal strap. Bailey had lingered to play with the puppy and pick out a newly released mystery to buy. Now Chloe was here with a nice, long list of books, and Pages was teeming with shoppers.

And Hoyt Bradley had *kissed* her last night.

What was that wonderful Bible passage in the twenty-third psalm? *My cup runneth over.* That was exactly how Anna felt right now, as if the life she'd been longing for had suddenly caught up with her and buried her in unexpected blessings. It was all wonderful and overwhelming—and a little bit scary.

She heard a thump and looked down to see that Chester had managed to conquer the trash can again. He looked up at her, a sticky note stuck on the end of his nose, his tail thumping happily, as if he'd done her a favor.

Anna laughed, and Chloe tiptoed to peer over the counter. She made a tsking noise behind her teeth. "I see your new friend is keeping you busy. I hope you're happy with him. I warned Hoyt that surprising a woman with a puppy might not be such a good idea, but you know Hoyt. Once he gets an idea in his head, he's unstoppable."

"That's true." Strange how just the mention of Hoyt's name made Anna's stomach flip over. "But don't worry. I'm *very* happy." Avoiding Chloe's eyes, Anna knelt down to gather up the trash.

She wasn't getting away from Chloe that easily. The other woman knelt, too, and restrained Chester, who was licking all the carefully applied makeup off the tip of Anna's nose.

"Good. I was worried about the dog, but I didn't argue too much." Chloe spoke softly so as not to be overheard. "I was too tickled to see Hoyt so anxious to surprise you. He's locked himself in his grief for such a long time. I'd started to think this would never happen for him again, you know? For some people it's like that. I'm glad I was wrong." Her voice rippled with amusement. "From the look of that kiss Mitch interrupted we were both wrong. I'd say you and Hoyt are definitely dating now, wouldn't you?"

Anna bit her lip, and her eyes locked into Chloe's friendly ones. "I haven't seen him since then," she admitted in a nervous rush. "I expected him to come by so we could talk, but he hasn't."

"Oh, he will." A smile warmed Chloe's face. "Don't you worry." She turned Chester loose and stood.

The puppy immediately went for the freshly refilled wastepaper basket. Chloe snagged it first and placed it safely on the other side of the baby gate Anna had rigged up to enclose the checkout area. "So there, you little monster," she said sternly. "Now you have to behave yourself."

Chester yipped sharply. He plopped his fat bottom on the absorbent padding and tilted his head at Chloe and the now inaccessible trash.

It was a perfect and simple solution. Anna shook her head. "Why didn't I think of doing that?"

Chloe laughed. "You have other things on your mind today. And speaking of that—" she nodded toward the wide store windows "—I think maybe it's time for me to leave."

Anna followed Chloe's gaze. Hoyt's work truck was parked by the curb just outside the store. He was sitting in the cab, with his phone held to his ear.

Chapter Twelve

Outside Pages, Hoyt listened for the tenth time to the voice mail message Dr. Mills had left on his phone.

"Hi, Hoyt." The normally chipper therapist sounded weary. "Sorry it's taken me so long to get back to you. That's fabulous news about Jess. Sounds like she's making steady gains. I wish I could come back to Georgia to do an evaluation of her progress in person. Unfortunately, my mother has taken a turn for the worse, and I'm not sure when I'll get back home."

There was a pause before the older woman continued. "I listened to your most recent voice mail. You asked me to be honest with you, so I'm going to be. On the one hand, I think it's wonderful that you're considering a relationship. If you were my patient, I'd celebrate this as a huge milestone. But you aren't my patient—Jess is. From that perspective, this situation causes me some concern. You've mentioned that you have a kind of up-and-down relationship with this Anna and that she's been making plans to relocate. We know that Jess has a history of reacting very dramatically when maternal relationships are disrupted. So, I suppose my question is, do you see yourself with this woman long-term? Because if you're not absolutely certain…until Jess's recovery has solidified, you might want to exercise some caution. But again, since I'm following all this long-distance, I might not have the full picture. Until I'm back in the office, I'd like you to consider allowing the school psychologist, Dr. Lee, to work with Jess. She's excellent, and I'm sure she'll be able to help you figure—"

Hoyt closed out his voice mail. He'd heard what he needed to hear.

He stared through the windshield of his truck. He'd spent most of last night thinking about what Dr. Mills had said. He'd still needed to hear it one more time before walking into the bookstore and facing Anna.

He'd landed himself in the middle of a mess.

For the thousandth time, his mind made a beeline back to that moment under the pine trees, to the feel of Anna's lips under his own. Why had he kissed her? He still wasn't sure. But what he did know was every time he thought about looking down into Anna's clear green eyes, so close he could count the little freckles spattered across her nose, all he wanted to do was find some excuse to kiss her again.

He'd had every intention of doing just that—right up until the moment he'd listened to the voice mail and heard Dr. Mills say *absolutely certain* and *long-term.*

If it wasn't for Jess, he'd risk moving ahead with Anna and see where that unexpected kiss could take them. But there was nothing *absolutely certain* where he and Anna Delaney were concerned. He sure couldn't risk Jess's recovery on the slim chance that a woman two shakes away from getting a PhD would want a long-term relationship with a construction worker who'd barely scraped through high school.

But he couldn't leave that kiss hanging in the air between them, either. He owed Anna more than that. He had to come clean and straighten this out.

Chloe Connor was exiting Pages when he rounded the front of his truck.

"Hoyt! What a surprise to see you here!" The teasing tone in Chloe's voice made it clear that she wasn't in the least surprised.

He nodded to Chloe with a tight smile, and the amusement faded from her face. She stopped dead on the sidewalk, her dark brows pulled together. "Hoyt? Is everything all right?"

"I can't talk now, Chloe. Sorry." Avoiding her concerned eyes, he edged past her and into the bookstore.

There were several people waiting in line at the cash register, but Anna looked up as soon as she heard him come in. Her eyes met his, and the electric shock of that connection jolted him all the way across the room. There was something new in Anna's eyes now when she looked at him, something soft and warm that hadn't been there before he'd lost his mind and kissed her.

Something that only made what he had to do that much harder.

But all she said was "Hi, Hoyt! Be with you in just a minute."

He watched as she waited on her customers. Anna helped them all patiently, but her eyes kept darting over to meet his. When the last shopper had taken his book and left, she sighed and gave him a bright smile.

"Sorry about that. Wouldn't you know it? Every single person in the store came up to the cash register at the same time. Not that I'm complaining," she added hastily. "I'm grateful for the business. If this keeps up, I'll be out of the red before too much longer." She offered him another smile. "I have you to thank for that. Bobby and Stork have been huge helps. And even Carl comes in to buy a book about every other day. Although I'm not entirely sure what he's doing with them. The topics are a little...surprising. Today he bought one on making origami animals."

Carl was probably using the things as doorstops. "Anna, we need to talk."

"Okay. Sure." She leaned over and unfastened a baby gate she had set up against the counter. Chester sprang free and scrambled forward to tug on the leg of Hoyt's blue jeans. Anna walked past him to the door, the light scent of her perfume surrounding him like a cloud of memories.

She flipped the sign to Closed and twisted the latch.

"This way we won't be interrupted. I was going to close up for a few minutes anyway. I need to take Chester for a walk." She closed the gap between them and tilted her head, her long curls swinging easily across her shoulders. "Which reminds me. I owe you another big thank-you, Hoyt."

"For what?" He wasn't really paying attention to what she was saying. Anna wasn't making this any easier, that was for sure. She was extra pretty when she smiled like that.

"For Chester. I can't believe the difference it's made, having him here. I should've gotten myself a dog a long time ago. I don't think I knew how much I hated living alone until last night. It's just so nice to have another living creature with me, you know?" She looked down at the puppy, who stumbled over the toe of Hoyt's boot and went tumbling across the floor. When he stopped rolling, his fat, hairless tummy faced up, and his pointed ears lay flat against the floor. He looked like a surprised brown bat.

Anna laughed, half closing her eyes and scrunching up her nose the way she did when she forgot about being prim and proper, and Hoyt's stomach did a double flip.

He wanted to kiss her again, right now, as much as he'd ever wanted anything in his life. He wanted it so much that he took a desperate step away from her, bumping hard into the bookshelf right behind him.

It rocked, nearly falling over backward, and Anna stopped laughing. As her eyes searched his face, the smile faded from her lips.

"Hoyt? Is something wrong?"

That was his opening. He had to take it. "I shouldn't have kissed you yesterday." He had to force the words out, and they sounded choppy and hard. "I'm sorry."

"You're sorry." The warmth drained from her face, and the tight lines he hated reformed around her lips.

It didn't matter. He had to keep going. He had to get this over with before he lost his nerve.

"It wasn't a good idea. I'm just not— I can't do this, Anna."

The silence stretched a heartbeat too long before she answered. "Can't do what, exactly?" Her voice sounded thin, like glass that would shatter if you looked at it sideways.

"Us. I can't do us." He knew he wasn't saying this right, but he was doing the best he could. It was killing him, seeing that look on her face. It made it hard to think, but he pushed on relentlessly. "If we started… dating…it could be hard on Jess."

The tension on Anna's face shifted instantly into concern at the mention of his daughter's name. "Hoyt, has Jess stopped talking again?"

"No. But her therapist is worried that she will. If we—" He broke off. "You and I both know we're too… different to make things work out long-term as anything other than friends. And maybe other guys can afford short-term relationships, but I can't. I have Jess to think about. I hope you understand."

Anna's expression didn't change, but her eyes chilled into two shards of green ice. "Of course" was all she said. "Don't worry. I understand perfectly."

She leaned over and gathered the still-upside-down puppy up into her arms. Chester must have sensed something was wrong. The little dog whined softly and then buried his nose against Anna's neck, burrowing under her spiraling hair.

"I'm really sorry," Hoyt repeated miserably.

She wouldn't look at him. "No need for you to apologize. It was a kiss, Hoyt. That's all. One *stupid* kiss on a very emotional day. It won't ever happen again."

"No, it won't." And that fact made him want to punch a hole in the wall. Instead he pulled his dog-eared notepad out of his shirt pocket and clicked open a pen. "Mitch's starting on the electrical repairs in a day or two, as soon as I get the materials in. He'll have to shut down the power for a few hours, so you should tell me when it would be the most convenient for him to start work."

"How much is the work going to cost?"

"Don't worry about it. Like I told you the other day, I'm covering the cost of the material and labor."

"No." She shook her head. "I can't let you do that. I already have that loan to repay you."

"Not the way I see it. I'm the one who owes you a debt, Anna. Please let me do this, and we'll call ourselves even."

She considered him for a second of two, her face unreadable. "If I agree, if I let you do this, then we'll be done? Right?"

His heart twisted. *Done.* He sure didn't like the sound of that. "Yeah, if that's what you want."

"And Mitch will be the one doing the work?"

"If that's the way you want it."

"I think that'd be best. Can he get them done fast?"

She wasn't bothering to pull any punches. Not that he blamed her. "Sure. Once the material comes in, Mitch can probably knock it out in about a week."

"Then all right." She shifted the puppy to free up a hand and held it out in his direction. "It's a deal."

He'd come in here promising himself he wasn't going to touch Anna, but if he didn't take her hand now, it was going to look rude. He enclosed her slender hand in his own, meaning to let it go as soon as he'd given it the required, strictly friendly squeeze.

Instead he stood there like an idiot, holding it and looking down into her face, wishing with all his heart that somehow this could've worked out differently. He found himself leaning closer, until he was almost back into the danger zone.

"I'm sorry I ruined things between us, Anna. I really am. I'm going to miss it, you know? Me and you spending time together."

She looked up into his eyes. For just a split second, he saw so much sadness in her face that he was ready to chuck this whole idea and forget everything Dr. Mills had said in that stupid voice mail.

Then her eyes frosted back over. She pulled her hand free of his and straightened her shoulders.

"It's *you and I*, Hoyt. Not *me and you*. I've told you that at least a million times. Now, if that's everything, you'll have to excuse me. Like I said, I need to take Chester for a walk before I reopen."

Anna finished her fourth turn around the town square. Chester happily jogged along in front of her on his red leash. In spite of the plastic bags she'd optimistically grabbed on her way out the door, the little dog hadn't slowed down enough to make any progress with his house training.

Which suited Anna fine. She and Chester could knuckle down on that later. Right now she needed to walk fast and try to clear her head.

She couldn't believe how stupid she'd been, building all kinds of meaning into something that was nothing but an impulsive mistake. Apparently all it took to transport her right back into the thick of a silly high school crush was a rescue puppy and one heart-stopping kiss beneath a stand of pine trees.

Anna picked up her pace until the leash between her and Chester drooped down nearly to the uneven sidewalk. She'd had enough of this. Maybe other people wanted to relive their high school days, but she didn't. She'd barely survived the first time.

Chester paused to sniff at the huge round planter full of striped pink begonias and cascading ivy set in front of Buds and Blooms. He raised his leg just as Trish came barreling out the door.

"Bad dog! Shoo!" She started to nudge the puppy away from the planter with one foot, but she caught sight of the expanding puddle, and took a step backward instead. "Eww. *Seriously*, Anna? You have a *dog* now?" Trish made a frustrated noise. "*Just* what you need."

Anna really wasn't in the mood for sarcasm. "Did you want something, Trish?"

"Yes. I feel it's only fair to let you know that I've lodged an official complaint with the city about the unsafe condition of your building. The clerk assured me you'd be forced to bring the wiring up to code." Trish was waiting for a reaction, but Anna kept her face blank. "Sorry, honey," Trish continued with a shrug. "It's nothing personal. I have to think about my own investment and, of course, my safety." She rubbed her baby bump.

Right. Anna remembered the delivery truck she'd seen parked in the alleyway behind their joined buildings early this morning. Two uniformed men had been unloading a colossal industrial cooler.

Anna had wondered where Trisha planned to put it. Buds and Blooms wasn't much bigger than Pages, and Trisha already had her space crammed to the gills. How was she planning to shoehorn that mammoth thing in?

Well, now she knew. Confident her strategically timed complaint was going to topple Anna right over into bankruptcy, Trish was moving full speed ahead with her expansion plans.

"Sorry to disappoint you, Trisha, but you're wasting everybody's time. The wiring repairs are already scheduled."

"They are? But—" Trisha faltered to a stop. The dismay on the other woman's face might have been funny if Anna had been in a different mood. "Do you think it's a good idea to take out a loan right now? I mean, sure, your business is picking up some, but you can't bank on that lasting. You don't want to dig the hole you're in any deeper, honey."

It was that condescending *honey* that did it. "I appreciate your concern, Trisha, but I'm not taking out a loan."

She should have kept her mouth shut. Understanding dawned across Trisha's face. "You've hoodwinked Hoyt Bradley into helping you." Trisha crossed her arms above her swollen midsection and lifted her eyebrows. "You've played your cards well there, I must say. I honestly didn't think you had it in you."

"I didn't hoodwink anybody. Hoyt offered to help."

Trisha made a scoffing noise. "Right. I asked Hoyt to get that electrical guy to hook up my new cooler today, but he said they were too busy. My husband had to get off work and come try to figure it out on his own. You always were a smart one. Playing up to Hoyt's little girl was a brilliant move."

"I wasn't *playing up* to Jess to finagle free repairs from Hoyt." Anna's protest came out sharper than she'd intended. Trisha's perfectly arched eyebrows went up another notch.

"Oh, I'm sure the repairs weren't the only reason. We all knew about that ridiculous crush you had on him back in high school, but I certainly hope you're not holding on to any hopes in that area. Take it from me. It's never going to happen. You're not his type. And even if you were—" Trisha shrugged "—Hoyt Bradley buried that part of his heart in Pine Valley Memorial Cemetery with Marylee Sherman. Everybody knows that."

A wave of hopelessness washed over Anna, and one thing became perfectly and completely clear.

She couldn't do this. She couldn't stay here and be ignored by the man she'd grown to care for—*love*, even. She might as well admit that to herself, at least. That kiss might have been a mistake as far as Hoyt was concerned, but it had shifted something inside of her. And she had no idea how to shift things back.

That was a problem. Unrequited crushes were bad enough in high school, but she wasn't in high school anymore.

This had to stop.

"You can sheath those claws of yours, Trisha. Like it or not, I'm bringing the bookstore up to code, and you won't be able to buy it for those bargain basement prices you've been throwing around." Anna paused, teetering on the brink of the decision that she knew needed to be made. Then she swallowed hard and took the plunge. "But I have some good news for you. If you really want this building you can have it. Make me an offer, a *real* one this time, and the place is yours."

Chapter Thirteen

Three nights later, Hoyt reared up on one elbow and socked his pillow. Then he flipped over and stared at the green numbers on the bedside clock.

2:14 a.m. He had a full workday scheduled, and he'd be shorthanded. Since Trish had somehow succeeded in strong-arming Anna into selling her building, he'd put a rush on the material order and asked Mitch to bump the bookstore repairs up on the schedule.

He needed sleep, but that wasn't happening. Instead, here he was, tossing and turning—and thinking about Anna.

"God, I'm having a tough time down here. I could use Your help." He spoke quietly. Jess's bedroom was right next door, and over the years he'd learned exactly how to pitch his prayers so she wouldn't wake up.

He'd prayed his way through plenty of sleepless nights since Marylee died. Although, come to think of it, he hadn't had so many of those lately.

Not since Anna had come back into his life. For a while now, things had been different.

And better. So much better.

Small wonder he'd stumbled into dangerous territory. Because Dr. Mills was right. It was dangerous—and not just for Jess.

He'd never been the kind of guy who moved from one relationship to another. Falling in love wasn't like flicking a light switch on and off, not for him. He played for keeps.

But there was no way he could ever hold the interest of a woman like Anna Delaney. She needed a whole different kind of man in her life, one she could have English-teacher-worthy conversations with at night while watching some brainy documentary on public television.

That wasn't him. He was more a tune-up-your-car-and-unclog-your-sink kind of guy. He was all wrong for Anna, and deep down, he figured she understood that, too.

Right now, Anna was alone and still grieving for her dad, and Hoyt knew firsthand how shortsighted that pain could make a person. If it could make the son of a drunk pick up a bottle, it shouldn't come as any surprise that it could also make a woman look up into the eyes of a man she could never love as if he was the one she'd been waiting for all her life.

He got that. In his head, anyway. His heart was still playing catch-up.

Hoyt switched on the lamp. He wasn't going to get any more sleep tonight. Might as well face that fact head-on, too, and make the best of it. He had those blueprints for the bank addition he needed to look over. He'd spend the rest of the night doing that.

Just as he swung his feet over the edge of the bed, his

charging phone buzzed and skittered across the bedside table. He picked it up and squinted at the text message.

Hoyt froze for one paralyzed second of disbelief before leaping out of bed. He snatched up yesterday's discarded jeans and shirt with shaking hands, his heart pounding like a jackhammer on steroids.

He had to wake Jess up and get both of them out to his truck *now.*

Anna's building was on fire.

Hoyt made it to town in record time. He pulled his truck in across from the bookstore, half expecting to see flames flickering crazily in the upstairs windows of Anna's apartment.

Nothing. The only thing flickering crazily was his own heartbeat. There were no fire trucks in sight, nothing.

Could the text have been a false alarm?

Please, God, yes. Let this be nothing.

Still, he wasn't about to leave without checking things out for himself.

He glanced into the back seat. Jess met his gaze, her blue eyes round. "Sweetheart, everything looks fine. I'm going to make sure Miss Anna's okay, then we're going to go back home. Just wait here in the truck, okay? I'll be right back."

She nodded solemnly. "Okay, Daddy."

Satisfied his daughter would stay put, Hoyt headed across the street. He was going to bang on that door until Anna came downstairs. She could yell at him all she wanted, but he needed to lay eyes on her, see for himself that she was all right before he headed home.

One thing was for sure. Later today he was going to have a serious talk with Mitch about this so-called state-of-the-art smoke alarm. The stupid thing had lopped at least five years off his life with this little malfunction.

Just as he passed the centerline of the road, the smell hit him. Smoke. At the same instant, he heard the first, distant wails of the siren over at the firehouse.

This was no false alarm.

He ran the rest of the way to the building. "Anna? *Anna!*" The door shook as he pounded, but there was no answer. He peered through the window. A shroud of smoke hung over the store. He could hear alarms going off inside, but Anna was nowhere in sight.

"Hoyt, what's wrong?" Bailey Quinn hurried up the street. Hoyt had no idea why Bailey had been hanging around her store at this hour, and he didn't care. Right now she was a godsend.

"Fire," he said shortly. "Jess is in my truck. Go stay with her, Bailey." He had to get into the bookstore, *now.* His eye lit on the set of concrete planters angled in front of Trisha's florist shop.

That little one right there would do. He heaved it up in his arms.

"Hoyt, the firefighters are on their way. Hear the sirens? Just wait." Hoyt didn't spare Bailey a glance. He was zeroed in on the window in the door.

"They're mostly volunteers, Bailey, you know that. It'll take them a few minutes to get assembled and suited up. I'm not leaving Anna in there alone until they get here. Go see to Jess. *Please.*" With all his strength he heaved the planter.

The glass shattered into a thousand pieces, and he reached through to unlatch the door. "Anna?" He pushed into the store, shards crunching under his boots.

Alarms were shrieking all around him, and small wonder. Smoke hung thick in the air.

Coughing, Hoyt turned his nose to his shirtsleeve and sucked in a breath. Bailey was yelling at him from outside, but he ignored her. Bailey Quinn was a practical woman. Once she saw she couldn't stop him, she'd go straight to Jess, like he'd asked.

He stumbled blindly through the store, knocking Anna's displays and tables aside as he went. He mounted the stairs three at a time and burst through the door into the apartment.

The smoke roiled heavily in the living room, but he saw no flames. Where was all this coming from? And where was Anna? There was no way she could be sleeping through this.

He didn't like what that suggested, but he shoved the fear away before it could take root. Anna was all right.

She had to be all right.

"Hey! Anna?" he called loudly. "It's Hoyt. Wake up! We need to get out of here! Your building's on fire."

He pushed open the bedroom door. A streetlight outside illuminated the smoky room. The narrow bed was rumpled, the sheets thrown back hurriedly, but Anna was nowhere to be seen.

"Anna!"

The only answer was a sharp yip from under the bed. He knelt and saw Chester backed up against the wall, trembling. The puppy whimpered.

Hoyt dragged the terrified dog across the floor to him. A big canvas book bag was slung over the bedpost. He snatched it off and upended it, causing half a dozen books to slither across the floor. He shoved the shaking puppy in. "Come on, doofus. Let's find Anna."

A rapid search proved that Anna was nowhere in the apartment, and the smoke was getting worse. Hoyt dropped to his knees and took a breath of the clearer air closer to the floor. Where was she? Had he missed her somehow? Had she already made it outside? “Anna!” he bellowed. “If you’re in here, please answer me!”

Chester yipped sharply from his bag, as if adding his plea to Hoyt’s.

“She’d never have left you, would she?” Hoyt muttered, his heart sinking. Anna was somewhere in this building, and if she wasn’t able to answer him, things were really bad.

God, help me find her. Please. I can’t lose her. I just can’t.

“Hoyt?”

The call came faintly through the walls, from somewhere in the storage space surrounding Anna’s living area. Hoyt thundered back down the bare-planked hallway to the storage rooms. The smoke was thicker here, and he jerked the collar of his T-shirt over his nose so he could breathe through the fabric. It didn’t help much. “Anna! Where are you?”

“In the big storage room!” She broke off with a cough. “I can’t get out. A bookcase fell in front of the door, and I can’t move it.”

“Hang on!”

Hoyt slung the canvas bag with the squirming puppy across his back to free up his arms. Jamming his shoulder against the door, he pressed hard. The bookcase resisted him. It must have been mammoth. He forced the door open an inch and peered through.

Anna was crouched off to the side, barely visible in the swirling smoke. She had gone low to try to breathe, but the smoke line was hovering only about ten inches off the floor.

He had to get her out of there.

"Are you hurt?"

"No. I jumped back when the bookcase fell over. I couldn't get the door open!"

"I'll have you out in a minute." Hoyt repositioned his shoulder against the door, closed his eyes and pushed with everything he had. The door grudgingly opened another scant inch. He took a breath and pushed again. He had to get a gap wide enough for Anna to slip through.

"Stop!"

"What?"

"The bookcase! You're jamming it up like a wedge. The door's not going to open that way!" That tense tone in her voice. He'd heard it before—in the airplane right before she passed out.

If she had one of those panic attacks now…

Please God. Help us. Keep her calm.

He pressed his face back against the crack, but he couldn't see the position of the bookcase from this angle. What he could see was a glowing flicker in the depths of the smoke-filled space.

Flames.

The fire buried in the depths of the walls was coming, and this place was constructed of hundred-year-old wood and stuffed with books. Once the flames hit all that willing tinder, everything around them was going up fast and hot.

He had to get Anna out. Now.

He summoned every bit of strength he had and

pushed, but the door slid open only another grudging half inch and then stuck tight.

"Hoyt, you're only making it worse! It's not going to work." Anna's protest was interrupted by more coughing. "You have to get out! I can hear the fire truck siren. Let the firefighters handle it. They'll have equipment for this."

They would. But that flicker... He wasn't sure they'd get up here fast enough. And Anna sounded even more panicky now.

"I'm not leaving you alone."

"You have to, Hoyt! What about Jess? If anything happens to you—"

"We're just going to have to make sure nothing happens to either of us, Anna." He swallowed hard. "I can't see what I'm dealing with from here. Can you describe it to me?"

"The bookcase fell on top of some books, so it's sitting at an angle. When you opened the door, it tilted it up so that it's wedged hard against the floor."

That wasn't good. But Hoyt noticed that Anna's voice sounded a little steadier, and that was a positive. At least he could keep her talking and distracted while he figured out what he was going to do. "Is there anything you can do from your side?"

"No! I was trying before you came here. I'm not strong enough to— Wait." There was a short pause that made Hoyt's pounding heart ramp up.

Please, Lord. Help her see something, anything.

"Hoyt, close the door."

"What?"

"Close the door. If you do, I think the bookcase will fall back to the floor and then maybe we can move it. I'm pulling out some of the books that have it propped up now." He heard her scuffling around. "Oh, these poor, poor books. Some of these are first editions! Completely irreplaceable. My dad—"

Seriously?

"Anna, now is *not the time*."

"Okay. I think I've got it. Pull the door back toward you. And if this doesn't work, you have to get out. The firefighters will have to handle it. Hoyt? Do you hear me?"

"I hear you." That much was true. He did. But no way was he leaving here without her.

He hesitated. What Anna was suggesting made sense, but everything inside him warred against the idea of surrendering this hard-earned gap without seeing for himself how the bookcase was positioned. What if this idea had nothing to do with that desperate prayer he'd just thrown up? What if this just made the problem worse?

Don't start thinking what if. Jacob Stone's warning echoed in his memory. *That's where faith comes in.*

"Hoyt! *Close the door!*"

He ground his teeth together and pulled on the brass doorknob as hard as he could. The door slammed back into place.

Silence.

"Anna?"

There was a resounding crash. "Ouch!"

"Anna!"

"It's all right. I had to jump up on the bookcase to make it fall all the way flat, and I twisted my ankle. Wait a second." He heard more scuffling. "Okay." Anna coughed deeply. "On three, push as hard as you can. One, two...*three*!"

Hoyt summoned every ounce of strength he had and slammed his body against the door.

There was still some resistance, but it slid—and kept sliding until there was a gap large enough for him to squeeze through.

He stumbled through the door—Anna was crouched by the end of the bookcase, her fingers clenched around its side. She'd been pulling while he'd pushed. She stood up shakily as he reached her.

"We did it!"

"We did. Now come on. Let's get out of here." Coughing, they picked their way through the tumble of books to the doorway. He pushed Anna through the gap and looped his arm around her waist as they stumbled toward the stairs.

She was limping. She was moving as fast as she could, but he could tell every step was hurting her. So when they reached the top of the stairs, he paused.

"I know you're not going to like this, but we'll move a lot faster if I just carry you. Okay?" She nodded, and he picked her up. "Put your arms around my neck and hang on. And while you're at it, tell that dog of yours to quit scrabbling around in his bag. He's scratching up my back."

"Chester?" Her hands clenched behind his neck. "You found Chester?"

"I found both of you, and now we're all getting out of here."

And then I'm never, ever letting you go.

Anna kept her eyes scrunched shut as Hoyt carried her down the steps. She'd managed to work one hand down into the bag where Chester was, and he was licking her fingers frantically. Her ankle throbbed and her nose and throat burned with the smoke, but she felt an overwhelming sense of relief.

She could feel the hard strength of Hoyt's arms around her as he moved through the store, and she'd recognized that tone in his voice just now.

Now we're all getting out of here.

That was Hoyt's go-big-or-go-home voice. And that meant whatever stood between them and that door didn't stand a chance.

She kept telling herself that over and over again until she felt fresh, cool air on her face.

Anna could hear the hubbub around her, but she didn't open her eyes. She just held on to Hoyt, even when she felt hands trying to tug her away.

"You can let go now, Anna. We're out. The paramedics need to check you over. Careful, guys. Her ankle is hurt."

Anna reluctantly loosened her grip and opened her eyes. She caught one good look at Hoyt's smoke-smudged face before a paramedic moved between them, shining a light in her eyes. She tried to speak but broke off into a fit of coughing instead.

"We need some oxygen here! Hoyt, step back, will you? Donny can check you out while I see about your girl here."

"I'm all right. Just make sure she is."

"That's what I'm trying to do. Ma'am? Do you remember me?" Anna focused her gaze on the paramedic. He smiled at her as he clipped some sort of meter to her index finger. "We met at the airport after your first plane ride. We're going to see about that ankle of yours in just a minute, okay? How are you doing? Are you experiencing any chest pain? Are you feeling panicky?" He patted her arm gently. "Perfectly understandable if you are."

She shook her head. "No." Amazingly, she wasn't. She looked over the paramedic's shoulder to see Hoyt. He was shrugging off another uniformed man who was trying to draw Hoyt away, presumably to be examined himself. Hoyt wasn't budging, his eyes laser-focused on Anna. Chester's fuzzy face peeked comically out of her favorite book bag, which Hoyt was wearing slung over one broad shoulder.

The man looked like a cross between a navy SEAL and a librarian. With a puppy.

When he caught her watching him, he nodded and gave her a thumbs-up. Anna's eyes suddenly and inexplicably filled with tears.

"Ma'am? Don't look over there. Okay? You're all right, and your friend is all right. The rest is just stuff you can replace. You haven't lost anything that really matters."

Anna blinked up at the young medic. He thought she was crying over her bookstore, which she could see burning in the background, as a host of gray-clad firefighters struggled with hoses and equipment.

He had it all backward.

She wasn't grieving over what she'd lost.

What she was grieving over she'd never really had in the first place.

Six hours later, Anna looked out the window of Hoyt's truck at the smoking shell of her father's dream.

She wasn't the only one looking. Pine Valley had turned out in full force to view the disaster. People were milling around everywhere as the firefighters rolled up hoses and conferred in small, weary groups.

To think that she'd been worried, not that long ago, about people knowing she'd failed at running her father's business. That was nothing compared to burning the place down.

"Well." Hoyt drew in a breath. "The building's still standing."

It was, barely, but Anna didn't need an expert to tell her that the damage was extensive. She'd lost everything she owned, including all her store inventory. The low premium insurance she'd been able to afford wouldn't begin to cover all the losses.

And her own problems were the least of her worries. Trisha's shop appeared even more badly damaged, and Anna cringed at the thought of the conversation she'd soon be having with the florist.

Worst of all, the disasters in front of her might not even be the most serious destruction the fire had caused.

Hoyt had insisted on staying with her at the hospital. When he'd called Bailey to check on Jess, he'd come back looking concerned. Bailey had told him Jess was perfectly safe, but she'd been what Hoyt had termed "cagey." And she'd been very interested in exactly when Hoyt might be coming by to pick Jess up.

He brushed off Anna's questions after that, but she could tell he was worried. And of course he had good reason to be. The idea of the bookstore closing had upset the little girl a few weeks ago. Last night she'd seen the whole place go up in flames right in front of her. There was just no telling what kind of emotional trauma that had caused.

Anna sighed.

"I knew coming here wasn't a good idea." Hoyt was watching her, his face grim. "You heard what Doc Peterson said. You need to rest and keep that foot elevated."

"It's just a sprain. Now that it's wrapped up, it's fine. And you needed to pick up Jess. Besides—" she glanced back out the window "—I'll have to face this sooner or later." She pushed open the truck door and stepped out.

The air still smelled strongly of smoke, mingling oddly with a faint scent of coffee. Almost every person on the street clutched a foam cup from Grounds of Faith. Well, at least the church-sponsored coffee shop was making a little money today. That was a tiny sliver of silver lining, she supposed.

Hoyt joined her beside the truck, Chester frisking happily at the end of a new leash. Hoyt took hold of her arm with his free hand. "If you're bound and determined to walk around, you should lean on me. No sense aggravating that sprain any more than necessary."

She could probably handle the pain better than the confusing feelings Hoyt's touch was stirring up. After everything they'd been through, her feelings about this man were all over the place.

She'd given up trying to control them. Right now she was just trying to survive them, hopefully without humiliating herself even more than she already had.

They surveyed the scene in front of them silently as Chester did his best to gnaw his leash in two.

Hoyt gave her arm a gentle squeeze. "It's going to be okay, Anna. Things look rough right now, I know, but God will work everything out. It'll take some time, but He'll get the job done."

Chester added a frustrated yap and plopped his fat

bottom on the sidewalk. Steadying herself on Hoyt's arm, Anna leaned over and tousled the puppy's soft ears. Things could have been so much worse. She had a lot to be thankful for.

"Hoyt, listen." She hesitated, but she might as well go ahead with the first of the numerous apologies she'd be making over the next few days. "I want you to know how deeply sorry I am."

"For what?"

"I should've listened to you the first time you told me about the wiring problems in my building. Instead I delayed dealing with it, and I put you in a position where you had to risk your life to save mine. When I think of what could have happened to you, and what that would have meant for Jess—" Anna broke off and shuddered. Hoyt tightened his grip on her arm.

"What happened here wasn't your fault, Anna."

"I knew better than to go wandering around after the smoke alarms started going off. I should have just gone out. But I wasn't able to find Chester, and I couldn't stand the thought of leaving him." Her voice wobbled, and she cleared her throat. She moved toward the café, and Hoyt walked beside her, shortening his long strides to match her halting ones.

"I'm the one who should feel bad about that. I'm the one who gave you this crazy dog. Chloe said he was hard to keep penned up. If he hadn't gotten out of his crate—"

"He didn't get out. I'd been letting him sleep on the bed with me. He always cried when I put him in the crate. And when the alarms started, of course he got spooked and jumped down. I never even thought about looking under the bed. In the past, he always went straight for that old attic area. He knew he wasn't supposed to be in there, so he'd hide back behind those bookcases. It was like a game to him. When I was trying to get behind them to look for him, that one fell and blocked the doorway. This whole thing from start to finish was my fault. I take full responsibility."

"Anna—"

"Bailey's waving to you from the coffee shop, Hoyt. You'd better go check on Jess."

The distraction worked. The mention of his daughter's name had Hoyt turning and looking for Bailey. The grocery store owner was standing in the doorway of Grounds of Faith, waving at them frantically with both hands. Anna's concern drooped into despair.

Something was definitely up, and she doubted it would be good news.

"Yeah, I better see what's going on." Hoyt's voice was level, but there was a grim undertone to it. She wasn't the only one worried about how this fire would impact Jess's speech.

"You go ahead. I'll slow you down. I'll come along in a minute." Anna tugged her arm free from his grasp. "Go on. I'll be fine."

"Anna Delaney, this is all your fault!" They turned. Distracted by Bailey, neither of them had noticed Trish approaching. "You *see*? You see what you did? Do you have any idea what you've cost me? My store is destroyed! And I have three weddings scheduled next week!"

Trisha's voice grew shriller with every sentence. The people milling around in the street stopped to listen. Anna wished she could sink through the pavement and disappear.

"Calm down, Trish." Hoyt reclaimed Anna's arm in a reassuring grip. "Getting all upset isn't going to help anything. You need to think about your baby."

Trisha's hand went protectively over her belly. "Believe me, I am thinking about him. He'll be going to college on your dime, Anna Delaney, I'll tell you that! I'm suing you. I've already made an appointment with a lawyer. I hope you don't have any plans for your insurance money, because you won't be seeing a penny of it!"

"Trisha—" Hoyt started, but that was as far as he got.

"Patricia Denise Saunders, that is quite *enough.*" Mrs. Abercrombie elbowed her way through the crowd. She looked at them all sternly through the glasses perched on the end of her nose.

Standing beside Hoyt with people staring and Mrs. Abercrombie frowning, Anna felt an unpleasant sense of high school déjà vu.

"Nobody will know what started this fire until the investigation is completed, and Anna lost every bit as much as you did." Mrs. Abercrombie spoke with her usual authority. "You should be sympathizing, not yelling at her on a public street. Now go into the café and sit down before you do yourself and that poor baby an injury."

"But—" Trisha prepared to launch a protest.

"Go."

Trisha huffed, but Mrs. Abercrombie hadn't lost her touch. After one more scathing glare in Anna's direction, Trisha turned on her heel and headed toward the café.

Mrs. Abercrombie waited until she was out of earshot before turning back to Anna. "Patricia has always had a tendency to overreact in a crisis. You mustn't take it personally, Anna. Nobody holds you responsible for this."

The sympathetic murmur from the crowd made tears prickle in Anna's eyes, but she had to be honest. "I'm afraid it *is* my fault, Mrs. Abercrombie. The wiring in my building—"

"Was not installed by you." Her former teacher finished the sentence. "And until we have all the information, we can't be sure *what* the cause was. No sense borrowing trouble. Count your blessings, Anna. Even if it does turn out that the wiring was at fault, well…" Her teacher smiled and lifted up her Grounds of Faith cup. "Maybe you can share the money in the Rebuild the Bookstore fund with Patricia to help offset her losses."

Anna blinked. "Rebuild the Bookstore?"

"Last I heard, the contributions were already in the thousands, and it's only been a few hours. Bailey Quinn is spearheading it. The church café is helping out, too. They donated the coffee and some pastries. And that little daughter of yours, Hoyt," Mrs. Abercrombie chuckled softly. "She can be quite persuasive. When she'd finished telling me about how that store had encouraged her love of reading…well, I had my checkbook out before I knew it."

"What?"

"She told me you had a good owl book." A woman spoke up from the crowd. "My grandson is all about owls now, too. Do you think you could order me a copy? I know you don't have an actual store right now, but you can still order things, can't you?"

"I'd like a copy of that one, too." Another woman elbowed her way to the front of the group. "And Jess told me they're studying wolves next at day care. Do you think you could order some books on wolves? Maybe some beginning readers? My nephew is *very* advanced for his age."

"Wait a minute." This time the urgency in Hoyt's voice cut through the crowd's babbling like a knife. "Did you say *Jess* told you that?"

"Yes."

"She's turned into quite the little fund-raiser, your daughter. She just talked me into buying a third cup of coffee," the elderly church secretary, Arlene Marvin, said wryly. "And one of Emily Whitlock's cinnamon buns. All that sugar and caffeine… I'm not going to sleep for a week. On the bright side, with all this energy, I might actually get Jacob's office straightened up for once."

"*Jess?* Jess is the one talking to all of you?" The incredulous disbelief in Hoyt's voice had Anna reaching out to give *his* arm a reassuring squeeze.

"Yes." Bailey Quinn approached them, her dark eyes sparkling with joy. "That's what I was coming over to tell you, Hoyt. Jess has been talking to everybody. All morning long."

Chapter Fourteen

Two days later, Hoyt paced a bright, apple-decorated kindergarten classroom at Pine Valley Elementary. "Why's Dr. Lee's assessment taking so long? Ever since the fire, Jess has been talking nonstop to everybody. What do you think the problem is?"

Anna was perched on a child-size red plastic chair, her injured foot propped up on a second one. "Try to calm down, Hoyt. I'm sure Mrs. Abercrombie will be back with good news in a few minutes."

He ran one hand through his hair and shot her an apologetic glance. "Sorry. And thanks again for coming with me. I know you've got your own stuff to deal with."

Since the night of the fire, Anna and Chester had been staying in Bailey's spare bedroom. Right now she was wearing a blue shirt with daisies sprinkled all over it and khakis that didn't quite fit her. Bailey and Emily Whitlock had given her clothes and other stuff, he knew. That was nice, but not having her own things still had to be hard for her.

"I was glad to come." Anna shifted her ankle slightly

and winced. "And don't apologize. Believe me, I understand how hard waiting can be when you're anxious."

Anna was still waiting to find out the official cause of the bookstore fire. She hadn't said much about it, but Hoyt could tell the suspense was stretching her nerves thin.

He was in a nerve-stretching holding pattern of his own. Ever since he'd realized how he felt about Anna the night of the fire, he'd been trying to figure out the best way to share those feelings with Anna.

So far, he'd come up with nothing that didn't sound stupid, even to him. And one thing was for sure, sounding dumb definitely wasn't going to work in his favor with Anna Delaney.

He needed to get this right. He figured it was unlikely Anna would feel the same way he did, but there was no way he was walking away from this now without giving it his very best shot. And he didn't need Anna all keyed up and distracted when he made his pitch.

He pulled out his phone. "I'll call the fire chief again and see if the investigator has turned in his report yet." Before he could find the number, the classroom door opened.

"Well, now." Mrs. Abercrombie came briskly into the room and shut the door behind herself. "The assessment's completed."

"And?" Hoyt froze in front of windows spattered with red apple decals, staring at his former teacher, the phone forgotten in his hand.

"And I must say, Pine Valley is truly blessed to have such fine people working in our schools. Do you know, nobody made the slightest murmur about coming in for this evaluation during their summer vacation? Not one.

It warms my heart to see that sort of dedication among our educators, it really does."

"Yeah. Me, too." Hoyt swallowed hard. "So how did it go? And where's Jess?"

"Jess is fine. I asked Dr. Lee to take her to the playground for a few minutes so that you and I could chat privately."

Hoyt frowned. That didn't sound promising. "What's wrong? Wouldn't Jess talk during the assessment?"

"Oh, yes, she spoke to us, and Dr. Lee saw no reason to think that Jess will stop talking again. But after a careful evaluation, we do have some suggestions about Jess's placement that we wanted to discuss with you. The kindergarten teacher she's been assigned to is quite concerned—"

Hoyt's heart fell. He opened his mouth to cut in, but Anna beat him to it. She'd managed to get herself to a standing position, and she was leveling a hard look at their former teacher. "Wait just a minute, Mrs. Abercrombie. There's absolutely nothing for the kindergarten teacher to be concerned about!"

"Anna," Mrs. Abercrombie began, but Anna interrupted her.

"You and I both know that Jess Bradley is a very bright little girl. In fact, she's already a fluent reader, and she's incredibly creative. And her vocabulary! It's amazing for a child her age." Anna ticked his daughter's strengths off on her fingers. "Even if Jess stopped talking again tomorrow, any teacher worth her salt should consider herself fortunate to have a student like that join her classroom!"

Whoa. Hoyt realized his mouth was still hanging open. He shut it. He couldn't have said that better himself, so he might as well stay quiet and see what happened next.

He had no idea what that would be. Anna Delaney was going toe to toe with Mabel Abercrombie. This was like watching Robin take on Batman, except it was the battle of the brains.

Somebody should have sold tickets.

Mrs. Abercrombie waited, one eyebrow arched. "Are you *quite* finished, Miss Delaney?"

Anna wasn't giving an inch. She raised an eyebrow right back. "With all due respect, that very much depends on what you say next, Mrs. Abercrombie."

Hoyt couldn't take his eyes off Anna. She was leaning forward, her green eyes glittering like an angry lioness protecting her cub.

And all this was for his Jess.

A flood of emotions rose up and swamped him, until he felt like a rowboat caught in a hurricane. It was a good thing Anna was handling the talking right now. He didn't think he could have said a word.

Mrs. Abercrombie shook her head. "And I thought Hoyt here was going to be my problem. Believe me, my dear, everyone at that meeting truly wants the very best possible education for Jess. But—" she held up a warning finger "—please don't interrupt me again— the kindergarten teacher expressed concerns that Jess is going to be *bored*." The older woman's eyes twinkled behind her glasses. "After all, during our assessment we discovered that the child is already reading at a fifth-grade level. I doubt she'll find learning the alphabet particularly interesting."

That got Hoyt's attention. *"What?"*

"It's quite extraordinary, really. And unprecedented.

Pine Valley Elementary School hasn't had such an advanced beginning student since…" The former teacher smiled and nodded in Anna's direction. "Well, you, my dear. If I recall correctly, when you began kindergarten, you were reading quite fluently, as well."

"But at a third-grade level," Anna supplied with a smile. She turned to Hoyt. "This is amazing news, Hoyt!"

"Hold on a minute." His bewildered brain was struggling to catch up. "Mrs. A., are you saying my Jess is smarter than *Anna*?"

"No, of course not. All I'm saying right now is that your daughter's reading level is higher than Anna's was at that age. It's simply a very interesting observation."

Interesting, maybe, but there was nothing *simple* about any of this. "I need to sit down." Hoyt fumbled behind him for one of the tiny red plastic seats.

"Don't sit on that." Mrs. Abercrombie quickly wheeled the teacher's chair around the desk. "It would never hold you. Sit here."

Hoyt sank onto the squeaking chair, massaging his forehead with one sweaty hand. "Reading at a fifth-grade level," he muttered. "My Jess."

"That's why the assessment team is recommending that Jess enter our new Challenge program. She'll be in the regular kindergarten classroom half the day. The other half, she'll be pulled out for enrichment activities more suitable to her personal academic level. I assume you're agreeable to this arrangement?"

Hoyt managed a nod. "Yeah, I guess so."

"Good. Now, I'll go get the forms you'll need to sign."

"I'm sorry if I seemed rude, Mrs. Abercrombie."

Anna spoke up quickly. "I should have listened to everything you had to say before I got upset."

"That's quite all right, my dear. I understand. And if I may say so, you're very blessed, Hoyt, to have Anna here helping you advocate for Jess." The older woman smiled. "She'll be able to empathize with so many of the challenges Jess may encounter. I have a feeling she's going to be a valuable resource for both you and your daughter going forward."

After Mrs. Abercrombie left the room, Anna took a quick step in his direction. For a second he thought she was about to hug him, but then she stopped awkwardly. "Hoyt, this is wonderful news! I think Jess is going to love being in the enrichment program, and—" She paused and frowned. "What are you doing?"

"Making that call to the fire chief."

"Don't worry about that right now! I can wait."

"I can't." That almost-hug had decided it for him. He wasn't waiting any longer to get things settled between them, and Anna was going to need to know where she stood with the fire investigation before she'd be ready to listen to what he had to say. "Tim? It's Hoyt. What's the news on the bookstore fire? Has the investigator gotten back to you? Okay, good. No, just give me the gist."

He listened, watching Anna's expression tense as she searched his face for clues. "Got it. Thanks." He disconnected the call and smiled. "The fire wasn't your fault."

Anna drew in a sharp breath. "Are they *sure*, Hoyt? If it wasn't the wiring, what on earth happened?"

"Trisha's new cooler happened. Apparently her husband goofed up when he was installing it, and the motor overheated."

"The fire was *Trisha's* fault?"

"It looks that way."

"Oh, my! That's such a relief. For me, anyway. I can't imagine Trisha's going to be happy about this. I really hope it doesn't affect her pregnancy. I remember the professor in my Human Growth and Development class saying once that—"

She'd started talking about professors and classes. If he didn't head her off fast, she'd be quoting books and this whole conversation he was trying to have would be derailed before it even got started.

"Anna, Mrs. Abercrombie will be coming back with those forms in a few minutes, and I really need to ask you a question before she does."

Anna stopped in midsentence and blinked at him. "Okay. Sure. What is it?"

"Do you want to stay in Pine Valley and rebuild the bookstore? I need to know."

There was a brief silence, heavy with all the things that had hung between them since the fire.

Then, "Why?" Anna asked finally. "Why do you need to know, Hoyt?"

He should've known Anna wouldn't make this easy on him. "I think maybe you know why."

"I think maybe you need to tell me."

Hoyt rose and walked toward the big windows. "On second thought, maybe we shouldn't have this talk here," he muttered. "Schools always make me squirrelly."

"You're in a kindergarten classroom, Hoyt." Wry frustration rippled in Anna's voice. "If five-year-olds can handle being here, I'm pretty sure you can."

In spite of the nerves jostling around in his gut, Hoyt chuckled.

Man, he loved that about Anna Delaney. She didn't hand out sympathy like breath mints. Try to sneak something by Anna, and she'd just shoot you an annoyed look and throw a flag on the play.

But underneath all that, down deep where it really counted, she had one of the best and truest hearts he'd ever known.

"Okay, then. Have it your way. We'll do this right here, right now." He crossed the room to where she was standing. He held out his hands, and after a second she put her fingers in his. "Listen to me, Anna. I can rebuild that bookstore for you, a lot better than it ever was." He paused, but in fairness to her, he had to paint the whole picture. "Or, you could take the insurance money and go back to college, if that's what you'd rather do. It's your choice. But I need to know. What do you *really* want?"

He was so keyed up waiting for her answer that it felt like forever before she whispered, "I don't know."

He raised his eyebrows. "Well, those are three words I don't think I've ever heard you say before."

The gibe worked. A flash of the old Annatude flickered in her eyes. "Not funny, Bradley. And anyway, you're not playing fair. That's an impossible question for somebody to answer on the spur of the moment."

"I think it's a very simple question."

"Oh, you do, do you? Well, then tell me this. What do *you* really want?"

He didn't respond right away. He couldn't, not with those green eyes fastened onto his. A man could lose himself in Anna's eyes if he wasn't careful.

Hoyt had never been all that good at being careful.

"See there?" Anna made an attempt at a laugh. "You don't know, either."

"Oh, yes, I do. This." He leaned forward and cupped a hand under her cheek. Her eyes widened. "I want this."

And he kissed her.

When he lifted his mouth from hers, her eyes fluttered open again, and he saw he'd been wrong all along.

Anna's eyes were a whole different shade than he'd always thought. They weren't ice green at all. They were the green of tropical oceans, of warm and gentle places that he'd always wanted to see for himself but never actually had. Places where people went to be together and alone all at the same time.

Honeymoon-type places.

"Wh-why?" She had some trouble getting her question out. He understood. His own pulse wouldn't have been jumping any harder if he'd been balancing himself on a steel beam a hundred feet up in the air.

On one foot.

So this was it. His do-it-right-or-die-trying moment. He'd fumbled more than his share of these.

Please, God. This is serious stuff right here. Let me get it right this time. Let me say the right things, the sweet things, the things a man should tell the woman he loves at a time like this.

But then he looked back into her eyes. There was a soft, clouded wonder in them that made something he'd buried deep in his heart wake up and sing out like a choir on Easter Sunday.

The joy was overwhelming. And he just couldn't help it. He grinned down at her. "*Why?* Why did I kiss you? You don't already know? Well then, that proves what I've been saying all along, doesn't it? Books are way overrated."

Anna's eyes widened and then narrowed. "You seriously want to pick a fight with me about reading? *Now?*"

"Come on now, Anna. You have to give me this one. How many romance books have you read in your lifetime? Like a million, right?"

"Not a *million*, for crying out loud. Some."

"*Plenty.* And even after reading all those books, you still can't tell when the man standing in front of you is head over heels in love with you." His voice shook a little on that last part, and he had to whisper the rest of it. "It's true. I love you, Anna, with everything that's in me. I do."

Anna stared at him.

It was the oddest thing. She knew the Bible said that hope deferred made a heart sick. Apparently hope realized made your knees turn to jelly.

Hoyt Bradley was in love with her.

"I thought—I thought you said you couldn't be in a relationship because of Jess."

"I said I couldn't be in a short-term relationship." If she hadn't been watching him so closely, she'd have missed the change in his face. His expression went from gentle to guarded in a split second. "That hasn't changed, Anna. I have to be straight with you. I know—" He stumbled to a stop in midsentence but for once, Anna had no words to offer.

She just had to stand there and wait him out.

He freed one hand and raked it roughly through his hair. Then he reclaimed her hands and started again. "Nobody has to tell me that I'm not the kind of man you saw yourself ending up with, Anna. I never went to college, I have a bad habit of using books for coasters, and if you sit me down at a table with more than one fork, you'd better hand me a cheat sheet because I'm going to be clueless. I'm all wrong for you. I may not have a bunch of letters after my name, but at least I know that much."

Hope kindled its sweet, incredulous glow in Anna's heart. "I really hope there's a *but* coming after all that," she prompted gently.

"But, Anna, I love you like fury." The words tumbled out in a clumsy rush. "I may not be even close to what you're looking for, and that's really not fair because you're absolutely everything I want. You're strong and sweet. You're smart and kind. And I know you're not going to believe me when I tell you this, but you're so beautiful you knock the breath right out of me." He leaned forward and traced a finger down the side of her cheek. "All those things you hate about yourself? This gorgeous, crazy hair you're always fighting with, the freckles on your nose, those eyes of yours… Those are the things that *make* you beautiful. You never had to try so hard to be perfect, Anna. You already are."

The words were unbelievable, but sincerity thrummed in Hoyt's voice. He meant what he was saying.

"Hoyt, I—" The hope in her heart was burning so strongly now that she desperately needed to put some of what she was feeling into words.

But Hoyt shifted his index finger until it rested very gently on her lips. She could feel it vibrating just the tiniest bit.

It was so strange. Hoyt was shaking.

And *nothing* scared Hoyt Bradley.

"You'd better let me get this out. If I don't say the rest of this now, I'm going to lose my nerve. You've got to be *sure*, Anna. I'm playing for keeps here. If you can't see a long-term future with an ordinary guy like me, and I wouldn't blame you if you didn't, then I need to know up front because—"

Enough was enough. Anna spoke from behind Hoyt's finger. "Fair warning, Hoyt. You may want to move your finger. Because if you start up again with that nonsense about how wrong you are for me, I might just bite it clean off."

The shocked look on his face was priceless. Then, just as she'd hoped, the worry lines eased into humor. He prudently removed his finger and grinned at her. "Is that right?"

"It most certainly is." She tried to keep her face stern, but her lips kept betraying her by tipping upward. "It's ridiculous, really, the way you underestimate yourself. I mean, *look* at you. You're a successful businessman, you're an incredible dad, not to mention you're so good-looking it's not even *fair*. That smile of yours should come with a warning label."

He cocked an eyebrow at her. "Keep going. This is getting interesting."

She made a face. "On the negative side, you're an awful tease, and you're not nearly as funny as you think you are. But I have to say, on the whole, deep down, you're just—" for the first time her voice cracked "—you're just the kindest, strongest, gentlest man in the whole wide world, and the idea that any woman wouldn't fall in love with you is absolutely—" She was going to say *ridiculous*, but that didn't begin to cover it. After a second, she gave up searching for the right word for how crazy that idea was and just shrugged mutely.

Maybe sometimes finding the right words just didn't

matter all that much. After all, Hoyt wasn't saying anything right now, but he was looking into her eyes in a way that said everything just perfectly.

"Here's the thing, Anna." There was a new tone in Hoyt's voice that had her pulse tripping so crazily she wasn't sure any blood was actually making it up to her brain. She was finding it hard to think about anything except that look in Hoyt's eyes. "I hope you mean all that. Because I'm not in love with *any woman.* I'm in love with you. So I need to know. Have *you* fallen in love with me?"

She knew she should make him wait, prolong the moment, the way the heroines always did in the best movie love scenes.

Instead her eyes teared up, and she could feel her nose starting to run a little. "Oh, *yes.*" The words stumbled out along with a sobby little hiccup. "Yes, I love you, Hoyt." She sniffled, and the sound was the most unromantic thing in the world. "A whole, whole lot."

The words weren't perfect. And she couldn't have cared less.

He squeezed her fingers tight. "For keeps, Anna?"

She nodded. "For keeps."

The joy that spread across his face was contagious. She could feel it beaming on her face, too. For a second they just smiled goofily at each other. Then Hoyt leaned forward and kissed her again, gently.

He drew a few inches back, his hazel eyes looking deeply into hers, questioning. Double-checking.

"This is it then, right? For both of us? From here on out, we're a team. Me and you."

Bless the man, he sounded so uncertain. He still

couldn't quite believe she meant it, and somehow that made her mean it even more.

"Yes, Hoyt. That's right. We're a team." She smiled up at him. "Me and you."

Epilogue

A chilly winter rain pelted the sidewalk, and Anna Bradley had to sidestep puddles as she hurried from her car to the shelter of her freshly reopened bookstore.

She didn't care.

The weather could be just as dreary as it wanted to be. Nothing could dampen her joy today.

The store was so crowded that she had to open the door in small nudges to edge people away from the display of audiobooks she had close to the door. Those were turning out to be popular; she'd better relocate them to a more spacious area.

If she could find one.

"Anna! There you are!" Mrs. Abercrombie angled her sparse frame to slide through the milling crowd. She made an apologetic gesture. "I'm just going to start off by saying I'm so sorry. I'm afraid this chaos is all my fault. When I mentioned I was bringing my after-school literacy class to tour the bookstore, all the other instructors asked to come along. I'm afraid we've over-whelmed your poor new assistant."

Anna glanced toward the register as she shrugged

off her coat. A long line of customers stretched nearly halfway down the length of the newly expanded store. Carlie was hurriedly ringing up purchase after purchase, and she cast a desperate look in her employer's direction.

Help, she mouthed.

Anna offered an encouraging smile and held up one finger. *In a minute.*

"I may as well make my full confession while I've got your ear. I'm sorry to say one of my students had a contraband chocolate pudding pack in his pocket. He took off his jacket and sat on it in the children's area—"

"Please don't worry about it."

"It was quite a *lot* of pudding, I'm afraid. And all over that lovely brand-new rug."

Anna laughed. "Good. That's the only thing wrong with this store right now. Everything's just a little too perfect. A few chocolate stains and some grubby fingerprints are just what we need. I really want people to feel at home here."

"Well." Her former teacher arched a thoughtful eyebrow. "I'm glad to hear you say that. Although it looks to me like people are feeling pretty comfortable here already. I admit, when I heard you were taking over the space next door, I worried that Pages would lose its cozy feel. But it really hasn't, has it?"

"No." Anna scanned her new domain with mingled gratitude and pride.

When Trisha had heard the results of the fire chief's investigation, she'd quickly dropped her lawsuit. Then she'd offered to sell her damaged building to Anna for a surprisingly reasonable price.

That wasn't the end of the surprises, either. It was

amazing what an insurance settlement, a lot of community support and a handy husband could accomplish in just a few short months.

Pages, now renamed Turn the Page, was absolutely beautiful.

Honey-colored bookcases lined the walls, stuffed with an array of tempting books that were constantly in need of replenishing. Colorful and attractive displays scattered here and there announced new releases and upcoming community events. Comfy armchairs invited readers to linger, and the seating areas were artfully angled to encourage quiet conversations.

Mrs. Abercrombie slipped one arm around Anna's waist and gave her a squeeze. "Your father would have been so pleased."

"Yes, I honestly think he would," Anna agreed, her voice wobbling.

"Oh, my dear, I'm so sorry. I didn't mean to make you cry."

Anna flapped one reassuring hand as she wiped her cheeks with the other. "Happy tears, Mrs. A. Happy tears." And maybe…hormonal ones.

That reminded her.

"Where's Hoyt?"

"Over there, listening to Jess read aloud to some of my students. She's been chattering up a storm for months now, but I don't think he'll ever get enough of hearing that child's voice." Mrs. Abercrombie breathed out a happy sigh. "The Lord has done some amazing things in this place, Anna."

"Yes, He has!" Anna gave her teacher a quick hug before heading off in search of her husband.

Her heart hammered with happy anticipation as she

sidled through the crowded store toward the children's area. Just as Mrs. Abercrombie had said, Hoyt was lingering on the edge of a sea of cross-legged children, toying absently with the tape measure he held in his hand as he listened to his daughter read aloud in a clear, lilting voice.

Anna had planned out just how she'd tell him the news. She'd pull him into the storeroom, and she'd hand him the tiny ultrasound picture she had tucked in her pocket. And she'd say—

He turned before she'd quite reached him, and a grin—the one that never failed to stop her pulse in its tracks—lit up his face.

"So?" He reached down and tipped up her chin, his hazel eyes searching hers. "What did Doc Peterson say?"

"*Hoyt!* How'd you know that's where I went?"

"Abel saw you ducking in the office and mentioned it when he came by with Emily and the twins. Emily swatted him, so I figured something was up. At least I hoped something was up." He paused, waiting. "I'm dying here, Anna. Have mercy on a guy. *Is* something up?"

Anna couldn't help it. The love and hope she saw on Hoyt's face made her insides go all gooey, and she couldn't help smiling. "Apparently so. Why don't we go somewhere private so we can talk about—"

That was all she got out before the metal tape measure in Hoyt's hand hit the floor with a loud clatter. Her husband swept her up in his arms and swung her around with a whoop that echoed through the store.

Chester left his post by Jess's side and ran over, scampering in a circle around them with ear-piercing yaps.

As he set her down gently, Anna's cheeks were flaming. Every eye in the store was on them. "Hoyt!" she whispered, "I had this all planned! This was supposed to be a really sweet, really *private* moment."

"Sorry." He didn't look a bit sorry. In fact, the man was grinning from ear to ear.

"Daddy!" From her stool in the corner, Jess shot her father an outraged look any librarian would have been proud of. "Why are you *hollering*? I'm trying to finish my story! Don't you want to hear the happy ending?"

"Sorry, baby. I guess happy endings aren't really my thing." Hoyt kept his eyes on Anna's, and the love shining in his gaze made her embarrassment blur into a soft, happy mush. He kissed her on the tip of her nose. "Happy beginnings. Now, those I like."

* * * * *

Dear Reader,

Hello! Thanks so much for joining me on my third trip back to Pine Valley, Georgia! I hope you enjoyed our visit there as much as I did!

This sweet little town definitely holds a special place in my heart. I had fun catching up with old friends—the characters from my first two books, *A Family for the Farmer* and *A Baby for the Minister.* And of course, I loved writing Hoyt and Anna's story. It features one of my favorite themes—how creatively God sometimes answers our prayers, often through very unlikely people and situations!

I'm planning to visit Pine Valley again before too long—I have my eye on our feisty grocery store owner Bailey Quinn. I think she needs a romance of her own, don't you? I sure hope you'll come along for that trip, too—you're such good company! In the meantime, let's stay in touch! You can reach me via email at laurelblountwrites@gmail.com and through my website, laurelblountbooks.com. Oh, and while you're there, don't forget to sign up for my newsletter—that way we can enjoy a visit every single month!

Looking forward to hearing from you, sweet friend!
Laurel Blount

COMING NEXT MONTH FROM
Love Inspired®

Available July 16, 2019

THE AMISH BACHELOR'S CHOICE
by Jocelyn McClay

When her late father's business is sold, Ruth Fisher plans on leaving her Amish community to continue her education. But as she helps transition the business into Malachi Schrock's hands, will her growing connection with the handsome new owner convince her to stay?

THE NANNY'S SECRET BABY
Redemption Ranch • by Lee Tobin McClain

In need of a nanny for his adopted little boy, Jack DeMoise temporarily hires his deceased wife's sister. But Jack doesn't know Arianna Shrader isn't just his son's aunt—she's his biological mother. Can she find a way to reveal her secret...and become a permanent part of this little family?

ROCKY MOUNTAIN MEMORIES
Rocky Mountain Haven • by Lois Richer

After an earthquake kills her husband and leaves her with amnesia, Gemma Andrews returns to her foster family's retreat to recuperate. But with her life shaken, she didn't plan on bonding with the retreat's handyman, Jake Elliott...or with her late husband's secret orphaned stepdaughter.

A RANCHER TO REMEMBER
Montana Twins • by Patricia Johns

If Olivia Martin can convince her old friend Sawyer West to reconcile with his former in-laws and allow them into his twins' lives, they will pay for her mother's hospital bills. There's just one problem: an accident wiped everything—including Olivia—from Sawyer's memory. Can she help him remember?

THE COWBOY'S TWIN SURPRISE
Triple Creek Cowboys • by Stephanie Dees

After a whirlwind Vegas romance, barrel racer Lacey Jenkins ends up secretly married and pregnant—with twins. Now can her rodeo cowboy husband, Devin Cole, ever win her heart for real?

A SOLDIER'S PRAYER
Maple Springs • by Jenna Mindel

When she's diagnosed with cancer, Monica Zelinsky heads to her uncle's cabin for a weekend alone to process—and discovers her brother's friend Cash Miller already there with his two young nephews. Stranded together by a storm, will Monica and Cash finally allow their childhood crushes to grow into something more?

LOOK FOR THESE AND OTHER LOVE INSPIRED BOOKS WHEREVER BOOKS ARE SOLD, INCLUDING MOST BOOKSTORES, SUPERMARKETS, DISCOUNT STORES AND DRUGSTORES.

LICNM0719

SPECIAL EXCERPT FROM

What happens when the nanny harbors a secret that could change everything?

Read on for a sneak preview of The Nanny's Secret Baby, *the next book in Lee Tobin McClain's Redemption Ranch miniseries.*

Any day she could see Sammy was a good day. But she was pretty sure Jack was about to turn down her nanny offer. And then she'd have to tell Penny she couldn't take the apartment, and leave.

The thought of being away from her son after spending precious time with him made her chest ache, and she blinked away unexpected tears as she approached Jack and Sammy.

Sammy didn't look up at her. He was holding up one finger near his own face, moving it back and forth.

Jack caught his hand. "Say hi, Sammy! Here's Aunt Arianna."

Sammy tugged his hand away and continued to move his finger in front of his face.

"Sammy, come on."

Sammy turned slightly away from his father and refocused on his fingers.

"It's okay," Arianna said, because she could see the beginnings of a meltdown. "He doesn't need to greet me. What's up?"

"Look," he said, "I've been thinking about what you said." He rubbed a hand over the back of his neck, clearly uncomfortable.

Sammy's hand moved faster, and he started humming a wordless tune. It was almost as if he could sense the tension between Arianna and Jack.

"It's okay, Jack," she said. "I get it. My being your nanny was a foolish idea." Foolish, but oh so appealing. She ached to pick

LIEXP0719

Sammy up and hold him, to know that she could spend more time with him, help him learn, get him support for his special needs.

But it wasn't her right.

"Actually," he said, "that's what I wanted to talk about. It does seem sort of foolish, but…I think I'd like to offer you the job."

She stared at him, her eyes filling. "Oh, Jack," she said, her voice coming out in a whisper. Had he really just said she could have the job?

Behind her, the rumble and snap of tables being folded and chairs being stacked, the cheerful conversation of parishioners and community people, faded to an indistinguishable murmur.

She was going to be able to be with her son. Every day. She reached out and stroked Sammy's soft hair, and even though he ignored her touch, her heart nearly melted with the joy of being close to him.

Jack's brow wrinkled. "On a trial basis," he said. "Just for the rest of the summer, say."

Of course. She pulled her hand away from Sammy and drew in a deep breath. She needed to calm down and take things one step at a time. Yes, leaving him at the end of the summer would break her heart ten times more. But even a few weeks with her son was more time than she deserved.

With God all things are possible. The pastor had said it, and she'd just witnessed its truth. She was being given a job, the care of her son and a place to live.

It was a blessing, a huge one. But it came at a cost: she was going to need to conceal the truth from Jack on a daily basis. And given the way her heart was jumping around in her chest, she wondered if she was going to be able to survive this much of God's blessing.

LIEXP0719

Looking for inspiration in tales
of hope, faith and heartfelt romance?

Check out **Love Inspired®** and
Love Inspired® Suspense books!

New books available every month!

CONNECT WITH US AT:

Facebook.com/groups/HarlequinConnection

 Facebook.com/HarlequinBooks

 Twitter.com/HarlequinBooks

 Instagram.com/HarlequinBooks

 Pinterest.com/HarlequinBooks

ReaderService.com

LIGENRE2018R2